P9-CLQ-951

IN THE
WATCHFUL CITY

S. QIOUYI LU

A TOM DOHERTY ASSOCIATES BOOK

NEW YORK

This is a work of fiction. All of the characters, organizations, and events portrayed in this novella are either products of the author's imagination or are used fictitiously.

IN THE WATCHFUL CITY

Copyright © 2021 by S. Qiouyi Lu

All rights reserved.

Cover art by Kuri Huang
Cover design by Christine Foltzer

Edited by Jonathan Strahan

A Tordotcom Book
Published by Tom Doherty Associates
120 Broadway
New York, NY 10271

www.tor.com

Tor® is a registered trademark of
Macmillan Publishing Group, LLC.

ISBN 978-1-250-79299-0 (ebook)
ISBN 978-1-250-79298-3 (trade paperback)

First Edition: August 2021

for the multitudes in each of us

Author's Note

This novella includes a depiction of a completed suicide. For resources and support on coping with suicide or suicidal ideation, please refer to this international list of suicide hotlines: www.suicide.org/international-suicide-hotlines.html. Additionally, some imagery may be triggering for self-harm survivors, specifically in the stories "A Death Made Manifold" and "As Dark As Hunger."

ANIMA CLOSES ÆR EYES and sees the world.

Æ borrows the body of a crow in flight. The two suns creep toward the horizon, casting long shadows from the floating islands overhead, shadows that cross the lapping waves of the Hăilèi Sea to the shores of Ora, plunging the city-state into twilight, even as sunset engulfs the rest of the world. The glow of the streetlamps in Tiānkyo, capital of the Skylands, underlines the gathering clouds. Sheltered by trees, Ora bides its time below, cut off from the rest of the world by choice, dark save for motes of light that escape through gaps in the canopy.

Anima releases the crow and plunges into the body of a tomcat padding down one of the city's alleys. Æ peers around a corner. A tall figure approaches, one hand wheeling an octagonal case. A black snake floats, weightless, above the figure's shoulders, sleek scales refracting sunlight into rainbows. Feline eyes narrowing, Anima swishes ær tail, relishing the feeling of it: an extension of ær body, vestigial in ær human form.

Cccccclacccccccccckkkkkkkkkkkkkkkkkk. The case clatters over the stones paving the street. The figure's skin is dark, rich, copper brown. Ser hair, a cloud of tightly coiled black curls, halos ser. Perched atop that halo like a crown is a gold headband, charms dangling from it like a veil. A gilded floral motif decorates the high plateau of ser forehead. Heavy, gold rings rest around ser neck; gold bangles clink against ser wrists. Ser glittering earrings brush against ser collarbones. A wind catches ser dark cape, billowing it out behind ser, revealing the brilliant, ochre dress se's wearing underneath, the material delicately patterned like a butterfly wing, shimmering in the slanted light.

Anima scans the figure's face and pulses the data into the Gleaming. No matches. Æ pulls back, observes enough data to establish the figure's gait, then pulses that data into the Gleaming.

Still no matches.

The figure's heels clack against the sett-paved street, sharp staccatos piercing the humming noise of the city. When the figure is a few steps away, Anima turns and flees, silent as æ came.

Anima opens ær eyes, giving ærself a moment to settle back into ær true body. Pinpricks of light flow out from the stem rooted to the nape of ær neck. Æ lifts ær hands, observing first the palms, then the backs. Lichen crusts ær nail beds, but the golden light of the Gleaming still shines through the cuticles.

The amniotic bath ripples as Anima sits up. Milky-white waves splash against the fibrous walls of ær pod. Æ traces ær fingers along the walls, then pushes apart the dense fronds overhead to reveal the darkness of the room beyond. Vines twist away from the pod and form thick bundles that weave into branches and cling to the scaly bark of an inverted tree whose roots puncture the roughly hewn slate of the ceiling as its crown presses against the floor.

It takes Anima a moment to notice the sound, but it soon becomes unmistakable: the same sharp staccato of heels from the city echoes down the subterranean halls of the Hub, accompanied by a smooth whir of wheels.

Æ isn't surprised, then, when the figure steps through the moon gate into the chamber. Se comes to a stop, pulling up the octagonal trunk beside ser as the snake settles onto ser shoulders, its muscled length twisting, dark eyes glittering.

"Hello," Anima says, watching the figure intently. It's been long enough since æ's spoken to anyone else that ær voice has once again become unfamiliar to ær ears. "How did you enter the city?"

"Through the Io gate, of course," the figure says, smiling. "You can check my registration, can't you?"

"I already have. Your record says that you came in through the northern Io gate."

"So what's the problem?"

The figure's gaze is dark, ser eyes like willow leaves, long and narrow, alluring and entrancing.

"I have no visual confirmation of you entering the city," Anima says slowly. "I only saw you exit an alley onto Anatoma Street."

There are all kinds of people in Ora, but the figure, still smiling as se stands before Anima, radiates something uncanny. Eerie.

Only when Anima looks down does the difference become clear.

The figure's shadow is detached from ser body. The gap between ser feet and ser shadow is about the length of ær palm.

"Who are you?" Anima asks.

"My name is Vessel." With an elegant swoop of ser arm, se gestures to the trunk beside ser. "I have come to Ora to exhibit my qíjìtáng."

"You need a business permit to do that," Anima says reflexively, but with little conviction. Ær gaze lingers on the trunk, made of dark-cherry rosewood, inlaid with mother-of-pearl and semiprecious stone, braced with bronze filigree corners. Vessel's slender hand rests on top. The dim light reflects a line of ethereal red off the wood and onto ser hand. Ser long, coffin-shaped nails are lacquered black, the fourth fingernail inset with a sparkling ruby ringed by a fine braid of gold.

"Do I? I'm not selling anything." Vessel lifts ser hand, another graceful gesture like water flowing over a stone; se cradles ser cheek in ser palm, ser other hand propping up ser elbow. "Would you like to see what I have?"

Anima parts ær lips, about to speak, but Vessel snaps ser fingers.

"Ah, I should mention," se says, "in order to see the collection, you must promise to add an item to it. Are you willing to do so?"

"I—"

Ær stem pulses. Anima's vision washes out into the gold of the Gleaming, spreading fractal-infinite through ær sight, plunging ær in the flow of particles and light.

fugitive

The suspect's face flashes directly onto ær retinas: masculine, vulpine; alabaster pale, eyes ocean dark. Anima takes note of the suspect's physical signature—gait, balance, tempo, pheromones, body odor, voice—and confirms receipt. The Gleaming retreats like a thousand-petaled lotus folding in on itself. It takes Anima a moment to adjust back to the dim light of ær chamber.

"Come back later," Anima says, cuticles and pupils pulsing with golden light. Before Vessel can reply, Anima sinks back into the amniotic bath of the pod, drawing the fronds closed after ærself. As the last of the glossy, green stalks interlace together, Anima catches a glimpse of Vessel's willow-leaf eyes lingering, watching.

———————

Anima borrows the eyes of a rat, scrabbles along the rooftops, claws catching on rough imbrices and tegulae scabbed over with lichen, tail held out for balance. Ær rat heart beats six times faster than ær human heart as æ sniffs the air, nostrils flaring and relaxing like semaphores. The scents of the city map out on a layer over the buildings and streets: humid, verdant air trapped under the canopy; sour whiffs of garbage waiting to be collected; methane from the sewers; urine and other markings from the animals living in the urban jungle; scallions frying in a nearby apartment; the sillage of someone's perfume; pheromone traces from all the people moving throughout the city—including the suspect's.

Anima seizes the note and follows its trail.

Æ slips through a hole in a roof and lands in an attic. Chasing the signature, Anima scurries through interlinked crawl spaces to cut through the dense neighborhoods, then darts out through an open window. Æ hops from awning to awning, clings to balconies and eaves, then makes ær way down tangled vines back to the ground. Peony Lane: Anima recognizes it immediately by the floral motifs on the bollards blocking traffic into a pedestrian area.

Anima releases the rat, then borrows a rock pigeon and takes flight. Ær olfactory map of the city shifts to accommodate the new vessel's sensory limits. Anima pinpoints the suspect's trace, then scans the crowds for the suspect's gait and other signatures. Within moments, Anima locks ær gaze on the suspect sprinting through the crowd toward the treetop walkways.

Anima releases the pigeon and dives into the body of a raccoon hunting through trash in an alley beside the entrance to the walkways. Æ launches ærself off the bin, scrambling for a hold on the setts as æ swings around to block the fugitive's path. The suspect skids to a stop. Anima scans his face, taking in his expression: panic, then a blaze of will. Æ snarls, fur puffed out, striped tail swishing.

The fugitive glances up. Anima follows his gaze to see an unfamiliar shadow flickering past the gaps in the canopy, too dark to be the Skylands' regular eclipsing of the suns. Anima hesitates, unsure whether to release the raccoon and investigate the shadow or to apprehend the fugitive while æ has the chance.

The fugitive makes the decision for ær. He darts

past Anima. With a screech, Anima leaps onto the fugitive—only to be flung off, hard. Anima crashes onto the stones, breath knocked out of ær. Æ twists and turns to get back onto ær feet, pressing ær belly to the ground as ær head spins. No use trying again.

Æ releases the raccoon and takes possession of another pigeon, intending to swoop in and slow the fugitive's escape. As æ rushes toward the fugitive, a point of golden light appears in ær peripheral vision: another node coming in as backup. A bubble of relief rises in Anima—then bursts.

Of *course* it's Enigma.

Anima flaps ær wings harder, hoping to incapacitate the fugitive alone. But the fugitive races into one of the elevators, foiling Anima's efforts to attack him. Angrily, Anima releases the pigeon and plummets into a squirrel clinging to a branch near the elevator platform. Chittering, claws scrabbling at the bark, Anima darts up and down the trunk, agitated as æ waits for the elevator to climb the three thousand units to the walkway. The pinprick of light in ær periphery becomes erratic, suggesting that Enigma, too, is leapfrogging through multiple bodies.

When the elevator doors open, the fugitive doesn't continue down the biometal walkway—instead, he climbs the branches of the trees themselves, nimble even as sweat drips down his brow and sticks his shirt to his skin. Anima launches ærself off the trunk, nipping at the fugitive's heels, scratching his arms. The stench of adrenaline emanates from him, protecting the fugitive from the pain as he ascends, brows knit together in focus.

Anima releases the squirrel and makes a beeline for a toucan farther away, its wingspan wider than the pigeon's, its brilliant beak larger and far more formidable. Stomach weightless with flight, head spinning with vertigo, Anima flaps ær wings with all ær might to fend off the nausea of such rapid body-hopping. Æ chases the fugitive through the top of the canopy and bursts into the bright sky. The twin heartbeat suns are on the far ends of their orbit, signaling the end of the month with their dimmer light—but neither they nor the floating islands cast the strange, unfamiliar shadow over the canopy.

A Skylander zeppelin floats over the treetops, ladder hanging from the gondola's open door.

The fugitive kicks off from the last branch, leaping for the ladder. Desperate, Anima pings the growing light on ær periphery.

hurry up

But Enigma doesn't acknowledge receipt of the message. Cursing, Anima musters up all of the toucan's energy and erupts with a burst of speed, vision locked on the fugitive's fingers, which are firm around the rungs of the ladder. By ær calculations, at the rate the fugitive is climbing and at ær own velocity, æ should be able to make it—

A man runs into the doorframe of the zeppelin. He kneels and grabs the fugitive's forearms to haul him up into the gondola. The fugitive pulls the door shut behind him; it clicks into place, locked from the inside. Anima cries out as æ slams into the door, ær claws scrabbling fiercely for purchase. Æ hammers at the round window. Filament-thin cracks spider out on the surface, but the thick glass holds.

Anima pulls back and bombards the window again. This time, the glass craters in a few tenths, not enough to pierce through the door, but enough to wedge ær beak in, keeping ær anchored in place even as æ beats ær wings to free ærself.

Frustrated, Anima shifts ær gaze past ær beak and into the gondola. The fugitive stands, dusting himself off. Tears spring to his eyes as he takes in the pilot, dressed in traditional Skylander garb. They step toward each other, the gap between them closing, until finally, they embrace, their love written in the fondness of their touch.

Shock ripples through Anima, compounding the force of ær final push. Ær beak comes free, hurtling ær backward. Thrown off-balance, æ drops far enough to see the zeppelin cross the aerospace border between Ora and the Skylands—the limits of Anima's jurisdiction.

Furious, Anima releases the toucan. For a moment, æ lets ærself simply plunge through the Gleaming, all gold and light, data and sortilege, physics and thaumaturgy: the place where the world simply is.

Æ lets ærself drift into the body of a gecko, if only to curl ær tail around ærself and sulk.

Enigma has the gall to show emself at that moment. Borrowing the body of a house sparrow, e lands on the branch beside the trunk Anima rests on, making it sway gently beneath eir feet. E hops over, cocking eir head. Anima's gecko eyes register the sparrow's fast blinking: translucent eyelids briefly obscure the bird's brilliant, black eyes. In human form, perceiving the sparrow's rapid blinking would be hopeless. But even while the gecko's eyes take in the bird, Anima can see Enigma's true face in the back of ær mind: delicately heart-shaped, surrounded by golden ringlets, eir eyes a rich, dark brown, eir lips pouty, eir nose small and flat.

"Where were you?" Anima snarls. Ær voice carries through the Gleaming directly to Enigma.

"I was at the other end of the city. You can't blame me for taking a while to get here."

"Bullshit," Anima says. "You could've borrowed anything. You were taking your time on purpose."

"What's wrong?" Enigma says, cocking eir head again. "Shit happens. People get away. What, are you having doubts over one failure?"

Anima doesn't dignify Enigma with a response.

"Or . . ."

It infuriates Anima that æ can *see* Enigma smiling, even though the sparrow before ær has its beak tightly closed.

"Are you surprised to see Orans and Skylanders having relationships—even though it's forbidden?"

Anima storms out of the gecko's body. Released, the gecko slips down the tree trunk, toes rustling against the bark.

Anima settles back into ær human body, aching despite the regenerative amniotic bath, ær stem aflame with data streaming outward in golden packets. Æ sits up, fingers aching to touch something real, something to ground ærself. Æ reaches up to push apart the fronds. There's not much æ can do to release ær agitation, but even a little exercise should be enough to let off some steam.

The last fronds pull apart.

Vessel is seated opposite the pod on the octagonal trunk. The snake flicks out a long, forked tongue.

"So," se says, standing and stepping aside to reveal the

carved rosewood, "have you decided whether you'd like to see the qíjìtáng?"

Anima grinds ær teeth. Some part of ær says æ shouldn't make any decisions while still irritated at Enigma and hurt over a failed mission.

But another part asks, *What harm can it be?*

"Sure," Anima says, letting more irritation slip than æ'd like. Then, after a pause, æ adds, "But I have nothing to give."

"Nonsense," Vessel says, smiling warmly. "Everyone has something to give. Take your time deciding what you'll contribute. You needn't offer it now."

Doubt constricts ær heart. But when Vessel opens the trunk, all that vanishes. Anima stares, awestruck, as the trunk unfolds. Clasps undo with soft *clicks*; mechanisms turn deep in the heart of the trunk, unlocking drawers that slide out with a clean *snap*, like a fan opening with a single flick of the wrist. Partitions slide away, revealing staggered tiers of shelves, each holding peculiar items labeled with cards in an elegant, handwritten script. The last piece to fall into place is a páifāng: twin ebony pillars rise up and mount a lacquered, wooden panel over the cabinet, inscribed in a language Anima doesn't recognize. Vessel says nothing as the last sounds die away, allowing Anima a moment to take in the cabinet's full size. It is now taller than Vessel and wider than ser arm span.

"Go ahead," Vessel says, bowing slightly and holding ser arms out to gesture at the shelves beside ser. "Pick an item, and I will tell you its story."

The sheer number of colors and textures and materials is a feast of sensory data that makes Anima's head tingle. Warped glass bottles, curiously shaped stones, bundles of documents, glittering trinkets and ornaments, dried flowers still scented with fragile fragrances, textiles woven from unfamiliar threads, taxidermied animals æ's never seen in the city . . .

Eventually, ær gaze rests on a doll—no, a marionette, bone-white, face painted like a skull with fine, floral patterns adorning her brow, silk flowers and pearls crowning her raven-dark hair. Her brightly embroidered dress flares out to just below her knees, revealing elegant dancers' shoes on her feet.

"May I?" Anima breathes, hands reaching out. Æ must have climbed out of the pod and crossed the span of the chamber, but æ has no recollection of doing so. Amniotic fluid pools at ær feet, but ær fingertips are dry.

Vessel nods.

"Please."

The moment Anima touches the fine stitching on the dress, the Gleaming reveals itself: golden embers spot various parts of the marionette. Of course, the maker of the marionette may not have called it the

Gleaming, but the qì lingers still.

"An excellent choice," Vessel says, straightening and taking the marionette in ser hands. "Please, make yourself comfortable."

Eyes still fixed on the marionette, Anima waves a hand. Vines and tendrils undulate from the upside-down tree. In moments, the greenery has woven into a bubble chair suspended from a liana, the inside of the round frame lined with lamb's ear and gently scented with sage. Anima sits cross-legged on the petal-soft leaves and folds ær hands in ær lap.

Vessel takes hold of the wooden controller. The marionette comes alive, standing up straight, hands clasped together.

"Let me tell you a story."

~

A Death Made Manifold

Past where the river turns to mountain lies the Prieta Desert, where the twin suns shine mercilessly and rain falls only a few times a year. Clustered at the base of craggy, cathedral rocks, nestled between thorns, is the town Agua Oscuro. The only train station in the three hundred miles between the coastal towns and the metropolis of New Makao is in Agua Oscuro. Still, despite its remoteness and relentless dry heat, Agua Oscuro is a good place to find work, and perhaps a bit of magic.

The newcomer steps off the steam-belching train, the only passenger rail passing through today. He has with him a handsome trunk, its fine leather exterior well cared for, its brass rivets shining. A thin sheet of yellow paper covered in intricate red lines peeks out from between the buckles. The newcomer wears round spectacles and dusty, leather shoes. He keeps his hair in a long, ink-black plait that drips down his back.

Sra. Vasquez keeps a boarding house in Agua Oscuro, where the rooms are simple but clean. Hàokōng pays for a month's lodgings and closes the door behind him as he settles into his room. He's only brought things that he can't purchase here—a couple photographs, a journal, a few talismans, outfits neatly pressed and folded.

A bound parcel takes up the rest of the space in the trunk. The yellow strip of paper, fixed on one end and free on the other, flutters in the breeze as Hàokōng opens the window. He doesn't undo the twine around the parcel. Instead, he tucks it safely away in the wardrobe. He doesn't open it in the coming days, but whenever he gets dressed, his gaze falls on the parcel, as if to reassure himself that it's still there.

He finds work quickly in the oil fields, vast swaths of land punctuated with drills plumbing the horizon. He nods at the other workers and makes an effort to learn their names. They're all men, and they all bullshit with each other as they work. They alternate between three languages and a melded fourth, the patois of the oil fields.

He works not just to pay for room and board, but also as a pretext to ask the locals questions and get a better lay of the land. He knows he's in the right town. He just has to find out where to go from here.

Oil greases his hands black. The suns turn his yellow skin brown. He quickly learns not to fuss over stains and to use soap with grit to wash his hands after work. When he gets home, he takes a wood-handled brush and scrubs under his fingernails to clean away the last of the black. He combs his hair and plaits it again, holding his own gaze as his fingers twist together locks of hair. When he's sure he's tidied himself up enough, he heads out.

The town square is bustling as the first sun sets, and it only gets busier as the second sun sets and the shadows grow longer. The town's main notice board is to one side of the square, pasted and pinned over with sun-bleached sheets of paper. A poster emblazoned with the single word WANTED at the top shows a photo of a gaunt man, his eyes hollow, his cheeks sunken, his stubble patchy, his grin skeleton-wide.

Octavio "La Muerte" Guerra
Wanted on counts of murder, arson, assault,
and kidnapping.
Do not approach. Report immediately to sheriff.

Hàokōng sits alone on a bench, contenting himself with watching people pass through the square. He glimpses the tail of a naga, patterned in dusky rose and sand tones, the markings different from the naga back home. A couple cuts off his view of her. Someone sings a romantic tune accompanied by a fiddle and a drum; somewhere on the other side of the square, street venders sell fresh fruit, roasted corn, and other treats.

"Mind if I join you?"

Hàokōng looks up. A brown-skinned man stands before him. He has on a wide-brimmed hat and a brightly patterned cover over his shoulders. The badge on his breast glints first, then the rich silver of his belt buckle, its cabochon turquoise vivid even in the dim light.

"No, sir."

The man chuckles.

"No need for any of that. I may be the sheriff, but I'm not too big on titles." He holds out a hand. "Anselmo Villalobos. But you can call me Ansel."

"Hàokōng Shì."

They shake hands. Hàokōng's gaze lingers on Ansel's

fingers, square and strong; he meets Ansel's eyes when he looks up. Ansel doesn't say anything, just keeps smiling, their hands touching for a moment longer before Ansel takes his away. Hàokōng breaks their gaze, his heart thumping.

"New to town, huh?" Anselmo says. When Hàokōng nods, Ansel laughs, the sound strong and good-natured. "Anyone can tell. You don't have the permanent squint that staring down the suns gives you. So—what brings you to town?"

Hàokōng pauses for a moment, turning words over in his mind. Finally, he says, "I wanted a fresh start."

Anselmo is sharp, Hàokōng can see that much in the way his eyes narrow, ever so slightly, as he looks over Hàokōng. He knows he's only telling part of the story, but soon his face softens back to warm and welcoming. He claps Hàokōng on the shoulder. Hàokōng stiffens. Different places have different understandings of touch, but for Anselmo to make contact with him so quickly and casually startles him almost to a blush. Ansel seems to notice and takes his hand away.

"Nice place for new starts," he says. A companionable silence settles over them as they both look out into the square. Then: "You planning on exploring much?"

"I suppose I'll do some sightseeing," Hàokōng says. A man a few feet away sells bouquets of round, fat succulents and spindly desert flowers. "The plants here are strange compared to what I'm used to seeing back home."

"Get past those spines and a lot of the plants will yield sweet water," Anselmo says, grinning. "Same as most of the people in these parts. Pricks until you get close."

Hàokōng glances at Ansel's face. He seems to be going for cordial, but Hàokōng's never sure, and he doesn't dare to ask for fear of the other man misunderstanding. He keeps his interest to himself as he chuckles.

"Not you, though."

"Eh." Ansel shrugs. "You'd be surprised."

"Would I?"

Hàokōng turns back to the square. A toddler chases a flock of pigeons and laughs in delight when they all take flight together. Words and snatches of dialog float through the air as people cross through the square, pausing for a smoke with each other. Golden clouds of pava smoke wreathe the view in a soft haze. When his eyes wander back to Ansel, Hàokōng finds that Ansel is watching him. His smile comes up a second too late.

"Something wrong, Sheriff?" he says. He tries to be calm, but nervousness churns through him. He thinks of the parcel in the wardrobe. He thinks of the heat rising throughout his body.

Ansel looks sheepish.

"You got me," he says, tugging his hat down to cover

his eyes. "I try not to do it, but I can't help it. It's my instinct to keep an eye on people. Especially strangers." He fixes his hat and offers Hàokōng a genuine smile this time. "But I mean no harm or prejudice by it."

A street over, church bells ring out from a spire visible from the bench. Not long after, a call to prayer echoes from somewhere farther away, overlaid with peals of laughter.

"It's a beautiful night," Ansel comments. The moonlight and the orange glow of the lamps carve Anselmo's jaw from the darkness: a smooth, strong line. He tips his head back to look up at the stars. For a moment, Hàokōng lets himself look, too.

"It is."

Ansel tips his head back down and turns to Hàokōng again. "Do you plan on going southwest of here?"

Hàokōng hesitates, then lies.

"No."

Southwest—that much he's sure of. But he still has to find the exact route. The desert's hinterland isn't charted on any map.

Ansel regards him for a moment, his eyes anywhere between golden and black depending on the dancing light. Feeling defensive, Hàokōng adds, "Why?"

Ansel crosses his arms and drums his fingers. His hands are crisscrossed with the shining lines of old scars.

He looks out at the square, but Hàokōng can't tell what he's looking at, if he's looking at anything at all.

"Most people come to Agua Oscuro for work. Our oil fields stretch beyond the horizon. And there's good business providing services for those to come to work here, too. They're all honest ways to earn a living."

Ansel pauses. He bites his lip as he considers his next words, his incisors and canines testing them before he speaks.

"But some people come here to make mistakes."

Nearby, a young couple touches their foreheads together. They kiss, bubbled in their affection for each other. A mother shouts at her child to come back to her. A game of kickball starts up among a group of teenagers, their shoes scuffling against the pavement.

"I've seen all sides of people," Anselmo continues. "The unexpected charity and compassion of a criminal—and the viciousness and brutality in so-called upstanding citizens."

With a sigh, he stands. The laugh lines have gone from his face, leaving him looking sterner and older.

"You're at a crossroads here," he says. As he turns, he eclipses a lamp, which backlights him like a halo.

Hàokōng remains silent, his heart thudding. Ansel hooks a thumb into one pocket. The revolver on his belt glints.

"I hope you make the right choice," Anselmo says.

He tips his hat. Before Hàokōng can say any more, Ansel leaves. As he departs, he greets a few more people. Then, a man holding a bunch of balloons walks by. When Hàokōng looks up again, Anselmo is gone.

Hàokōng pieces together the signposts by lying in wait and seeing who might be sympathetic. He eases into conversations, seeding unobtrusive comments and oblique questions, gathering scraps of information and clues.

Joe Rinaldo works on the oil fields with him. He's short and dark, with callused hands and a loud laugh. There is a hollowness that floats up within him, too, and it doesn't take long for Hàokōng to find out that Joe is still deeply grieving his wife's death. And he doesn't just grieve: He resents. He rages. He fights.

"I don't know if I'm raising my daughter right without her," Joe says. They're leaning against an oil pump, the machinery creaking under the suns. The oil well provides the only shade here when the suns are high. Sweat sticks their shirts to their backs. They squint despite their hats.

"Would you want to see your wife again, if you could?" Hàokōng asks, keeping his tone light, but Joe looks at him a moment too long, his gaze a shade too dark.

"There were times when I thought about seeing her again," Joe says, carefully. "I tried to for several years. But I gave up in the end. And, much as I would like an exception, perhaps the dead should stay dead."

"Perhaps," Hàokōng says. He offers chewing pava to Joe, who accepts it like a cow ruminating its cud. They don't speak for a couple moments. The machinery clangs. The wind carries distant shouts and commands from the ranch.

Hàokōng bites the bullet.

"How do you get to Cadena from here?"

Joe stops chewing.

"You really want to know?"

Hàokōng nods. Joe shakes his head. Hàokōng can't tell if he's disappointed or taking pity on him.

"Follow the Delicia River southwest, even where the banks seem unscalable—it's the most straightforward route," Joe says. "Pack money in different places in case of bandits. Watch out for rattlesnakes, especially the baby ones—they don't know how to hold back and will dose you with all their venom in one go. Fucks you up."

He starts chewing again, then spits.

"I wouldn't go if I were you," he says.

Hàokōng straightens up and steps around the machinery. Joe takes it as a signal to end their break. He gets back to work, too, but not before Hàokōng gets in a last word.

"You're not me, though," he says, smiling. "But thanks all the same."

———————

He uses some of his wages to buy a mule—more durable and less temperamental than a horse—and provisions. He buys a sturdy saddle and pack. He pares down his supplies to the most versatile of tools and equipment, pares down his food to dried fruit, nuts, and jerky. He bundles offerings securely with paper and twine to protect them on the journey, then packs them deep, away from sight and harm along with the parcel from his wardrobe.

He mounts the mule in a smooth motion, ready to set out before the second sun rises and scorches the earth. Anselmo is already waiting for him at the southwestern edge of town. He has both feet shoulder-width apart, his arms crossed, his sarape a dull maroon in the darkness.

"Leaving town?" he says, eyeing Hàokōng's preparations and the set of his jaw. Hàokōng keeps his expression resolute and neutral. The mule snorts. Hàokōng sways with its steps. The forthlight is fragile and delicate, rays of sunlight creeping over the horizon in washes of pink and blue and purple. In the half shadows, Anselmo's eyes go dark in their hollows. Hàokōng suppresses a shiver. The sheriff may be friendly, but that friendliness is practiced.

Hàokōng could turn back now. Call the whole thing off. Dismount and step close to the sheriff, ask him to show him around town rather than stop him at the border. If Hàokōng allows himself to, he can imagine a long path away from here, bright and weightless.

But then he remembers blood on his hands, the thundering revs as the Immortals pull away on their motorcycles, the diesel fumes choking his throat as his eyes water. He remembers the final, rattling gasps as he cradles the body to his chest.

"I'd like to get going before it gets too hot," Hàokōng says.

The mule takes a step. Anselmo speaks again.

"I can't stop you based only on intent," Anselmo says. In the rising light, with his shoulders drawn back to show the full breadth of his chest, with the shadows deepening his features, Anselmo intimidates even though he's on the ground and Hàokōng is up high. "But I would strongly advise you not to go."

"You know who's in Cadena," Hàokōng says. It's not a question.

"Unfortunately."

"I'm sorry," Hàokōng says. He turns his back on Anselmo, his shoulder blades pressing tightly together as he pulls himself to his full height. "I have to do this."

He can't see the expression on Anselmo's face or how he reacts. He doesn't give Anselmo a parting glance. Instead, he swallows his dread and urges the mule forward, but not before Anselmo speaks parting words that ring in his ears.

"So they all say."

———————

The journey isn't as rough as he expects. Having the mule certainly helps—he wouldn't have been able to navigate the more treacherous stretches on foot. It takes him four days to get to Cadena, where low, adobe houses sit squat on the horizon, bathing in the suns. The faces of the houses are wan, the cinnabar reds and earthen yellows all faded and muddled together into dusty hues. The roads are hard-packed dirt in the same muted shades. But surrounding the houses are plants in vibrant glazed pots that dot yards with color. Despite the heat, children chase after one another in the streets as their guardians sit on porches, several of them embroidering as they chat.

It doesn't take him long to find La Sombra. The people of Agua Oscuro had been hesitant to talk about her, as if her very name were taboo. But the people of Cadena seem proud to have a bruja among them. She offers them both protection and mystique. He only has to ask, and he's given directions to her. The people who live in Cadena can read strangers well, and they know not to ask why Hàokōng wishes to visit the bruja.

Her home isn't much different from the others in town. Larger, different kinds of potted plants, and a couple rogue tomcats yowling over robust barking. From beyond the door comes a hissed command. The dogs quiet down.

"Yes?" the woman says as she opens the door. Her dress is lightweight and finely embroidered along the collar, sleeves, and hem. Despite the haze rippling over the town as heat rises into the unforgiving sky, La Sombra remains clear, her gray hair, dark skin, and white and fuchsia clothes vivid against the pale yellow of the buttes and ridges and dirt.

"I've come to request your service," Hàokōng says. He bows deeply, then retrieves the offerings from his bag and unwraps them with care: a heavy bottle made of thick glass, its dark label finely illustrated. The spirits inside are a rich amber color, casting translucent, sparkling shadows onto the parched ground. He also presents her with a tasseled, stone talisman and a sachet of powerful-smelling herbs.

La Sombra brings each to eye level for inspection, as if she were a jeweler reading the facets of a gem. She nods after each evaluation, then says, "Well, you know what I like. Come in, then."

La Sombra guides him through her home, piled high with skeins of string and unmatched pieces of wood alongside half-used cans of paint and brushes with their handles spackled a million colors. Sawdust gathers in the corners. La Sombra leaves sidewinding snake trails in the dust on the floor, her strong, patterned tail extending from her floor-length skirt.

They exit into her backyard, where she sets the bottle down on a table and sits in a creaking chair beside it. Her skirt smooths over her in a single kneeless curve. Hàokōng finds himself surprised to see the lush green around them. Orange and lemon trees hang heavy with fruit. Wildflowers sway in the breeze, exhaling their scent. It is a well-loved and well-cultivated garden, homely and full.

La Sombra gestures for Hàokōng to sit. One of her dogs runs over, hairless and black, its whiplike tail wagging.

"Shh. Sit," she says. The dog obeys, looking first at La Sombra, then Hàokōng, who places the parcel on the table. La Sombra unties the twine with care and examines the slip of paper.

"You've made quite the journey," she says. Whether she is speaking to the parcel or to him, he can't tell. She traces her fingers over the flowing script and careful flourishes. "I presume this sigil is from Altyn."

"Yes," Hàokōng says. "You're familiar with it?"

"It would be foolish of me to not study the work of others who practice our craft," she says, her tone sharp. "Even if we may practice it differently."

She unsticks the sigil from the parcel, then peels back layer after layer of fine joss paper, which she places to the side to be burned with the sigil. Beneath all the wrappings is a simple, cloth-covered box, the crimson fabric gleaming.

She undoes the latch. A pile of bleached bones greets her, a grinning skull on top.

"Who is this?"

"My brother," Hàokōng replies. "Six years younger than me, and my only family since our parents passed. He . . ."

Hàokōng closes his eyes. La Sombra doesn't prompt him to keep going. She watches him, her expression unchanging, her eyes keen and relentless, as if she's scrying Hàokōng's every word and breath, measuring the weight of his heart against his mind.

"What do you hope to achieve?" La Sombra says when Hàokōng meets her eyes again.

He smiles ruefully.

"I will always be responsible in some way for my brother, and it was my failure that caused his death. I want to grant him back the life that was unjustly taken from him."

Bougainvillea climbs on trellises beside them. A few bees, lean and focused, dart from blossom to blossom. Somewhere in the neighborhood, a rooster cries out.

"It's been five years, and the absence is still eating away at me." He lets out a wry laugh. "I'm selfish, too. I don't want to be alone in the world."

La Sombra sighs. She stands, her skirts rustling. The dog follows her, tail wagging as it looks out into the handsome garden and vast horizon with her.

"If you give me one of his bones—any of them—I can make you a marionette of him, magicked and warded, as good a talisman as any," she says. "You can give him a second life that way. Tell his story to your friends, your family, to strangers. Keep him alive in your heart."

Silence passes between them. The breeze doesn't bring relief from the desert heat, only presses it closer to Hàokōng's sweat-slicked skin. After a while, he speaks.

"Then the skeleton would be incomplete."

"That's correct."

"You know you can't resurrect an incomplete skeleton."

La Sombra nods as she turns back to him.

"I'm giving you a way out, boy."

Hàokōng refuses to acquiesce. He fixes her with a hard

stare, his tone still polite but with an edge when he speaks again.

"I've come a long way to get here, Doña Sombra," he says. "I've crossed an ocean. I've crossed a desert. And I don't plan to give up now."

La Sombra gazes out into the garden, hands clasped behind her. Over the wall, a radio crackles to life with the tinny sound of music, accordion notes bright as they ripple through the air.

"He won't be the same person you knew."

La Sombra turns to look at him. She pauses just long enough to make Hàokōng tense. His response, then, is perhaps more clipped and irritated than he'd like.

"I expect that things will be different."

La Sombra crosses her arms.

"You know nothing. I won't simply perform the ritual for any child who comes wandering over here. Prove your dedication and bring me the Queen of the Night."

She waves a hand, dismissing him from her home. Her dog rises from its seated position, its brown eyes fixed on Hàokōng as it takes a fighting stance.

"She blossoms in the mountains once a year—around this time; luck favors you, at least—and only once," La Sombra continues. "Be sure to bring back the blossom fresh and before the suns rise. They will die with just a touch of sunlight. I can give you no further direction than that. Good luck. Take this with you."

She closes the lid of the box and slides it over to Hàokōng. She takes the thin joss paper and sigil to a pit in the yard. She starts a fire, places the papers in sheet by sheet, and sages the entire yard, shrouding herself in sweet smoke.

———————

As night falls, Hàokōng cranes his head back to look at the stars. Twice, as he travels up the foothills into the terraced rocks, he leads the mule away from the low, steady rattle of snakes hidden in the brush. He's not even sure what kind of plant he's looking for. A cactus of some sort, he knows that much, but several of them had blossomed during the day, and the rest show no hint of blooming. Many are gnarled and look dead, held in the dirt only by old roots. Irritated, Hàokōng wonders if La Sombra sent him on a quest simply as a way to tell him off.

But, if there's any chance she didn't . . .

He stops at a cave halfway up the mountain, the wind cool and refreshing as it whistles through the cavern: a nearly perfect circle looking out upon the valley below. It's beautiful, in its own way. Hàokōng is used to the lotuses of home, white blossoms rising out of muddy waters; the reeds lining the river; the tall and elegant trees that trap the humidity of summer as cicadas chirp through the night. Not these low, twisted trees, these spiny trunks and wide, thorny barrels, these strangely graceful flowers rising in fluid arcs over ring after ring of pointed, fleshy leaves sharp as teeth.

He could simply settle here, he thinks, after night after night of searching and finding nothing. He could simply give his brother a proper burial and move on. Truly start a new chapter in his life. Be an upstanding citizen with no darker secret than the loss everyone eventually faces. Maybe even get to know the sheriff better.

But a sense of duty, a debt he tells himself he owes his brother, keeps him going.

By the seventh day, he's already grown leaner with the meager provisions he has. His eyes sting with sweat, and his skin is coarse with salt.

Keep going, he tells himself.

By the tenth night, he's tired of stumbling over rocks with only the light of the moon to search for something that may as well not exist. By the eleventh night, the fatigue is almost too heavy to throw off. By the twelfth, he's talking to his mule just so he can hear a human voice.

The weight of his brother's bones urges him forward.

On the thirteenth night, he goes around the foothills again, combing the paths for any sign of flowering. Nothing. He's been stabbed twice by spines already, and he's spotted a pack of coyotes encroaching on his campsite. Cursing as he sucks blood from his wounded finger, he digs the rest of the thorn out with a needle. He might as well head back now. He hasn't made any progress.

His calves burn with every step he takes. Even when he's back on the mule, each step of the mule's hooves reverberates through his body and revives all the old aches he's been ignoring. He dismounts and ties the mule to a column of rock, ready to collapse into a deep sleep.

Then, he looks out into the valley and sees an unfamiliar patch of white.

It's far, but not unreachable. He mounts the mule again, almost knocking the pack off the animal's back in his haste. He pushes the mule to go as fast as it can, the patch's location shining in his mind. He pulls together the last of his willpower, gritting his teeth through the pain, until he rounds the last hill and descends on the patch of flowers.

Just seeing the blossoms would have brought Hàokōng joy, but their beauty stuns him into reverent silence. They're not unlike chrysanthemums, but their petals are silky white. He's been through this patch before, has seen it from camp for several days now, but only under the half-moon have the flowers opened, attached to what he'd mistaken as dead brush.

He collects one, two, three of the blossoms. A whole

bouquet, just to be sure. He can't tell what time it is by the moon alone, but sunrise will come quicker than he expects. He lashes the flowers securely to his pack, careful not to crush their delicate petals, and urges the mule to its full speed.

He doesn't sleep that night as he travels the entire distance back, only pausing for brief breaks to eat and feed his mule. As the faintest pink touches the horizon, Hàokōng dismounts before La Sombra's house and knocks on the door.

Several of the blossoms have already closed and wilted. Several more are limp and half-open. But one remains whole and perfect. Hàokōng offers it along with the box bearing his brother's bones to La Sombra, who greets him with a colorful marionette suspended from her left hand.

"I've done as you've asked."

"You have," La Sombra says. She adds, "You still have time to choose the marionette."

Her fingers claw around the wood. With a few deft movements, the marionette comes to life, stands a step before her, and dances to an unheard melody. The marionette's dress is exquisitely embroidered, her face and body still bearing the ivory-yellow tones of bone.

"My daughter," La Sombra says. The girl twirls and leaps through the air, her steps pitter-pattering like rain.

She dances gracefully, lithe and agile, eerily lifelike despite the marionette's simple joints. She leaps and performs one last twirl, falling into a heap before jumping back up and bowing to silent applause.

"I'm not turning back now," Hàokōng says.

The life drains out of the marionette as La Sombra gathers it back up and puts it away. Then, she takes the bones and the blossom from Hàokōng. She stacks the bones neatly and reverentially in the middle of the fire pit, the blossom tucked in one eye socket. She murmurs unfamiliar words under her breath as she circles around the pit, scattering salt and sage.

"I do not know what the consequences will be for you," she says as she completes her ministrations. "I'm sorry for that."

She lights the fire under the bones and steps back. Though Hàokōng knows the bones have survived one fire, his gut still churns, unsure whether his brother will only be further turned to ash. The blossom stays open for longer than he expects before its petals curl in on themselves and smolder down to embers carried away by the wind. La Sombra continues to murmur under her breath, her figure thrown into chiaroscuro relief by the open flame.

She hands Hàokōng a blade, her hand clasped around the sheath, the handle facing him.

"Life needs blood," she says. "It can only be given, not taken."

Hàokōng nods and draws the blade from its sheath, the sharp edge a bright line through the darkness. He looks at his left palm, the wrinkled lines inscrutable. He places the tip of the dagger against the meaty pad under his thumb and draws it against the flesh, hissing as the knife drags skin apart and rich, red blood wells up. He steps over to the fire and clenches his fist tight until the blood splatters against the bones and the flames become intolerable.

"What happens now?"

La Sombra nods toward the fire. Hàokōng's blood blackens as it spreads over the bones like ink, darkening everything in its path.

"White is the color of death," La Sombra says as the shadow grows. "The color of pictures and clothes and bones left untended and eaten by the suns. But black?" Her eyes glitter in the light of the dancing flames. "Black is the color of life. When you dig into damp, dark dirt to plant a seed or look at the space between stars, wondering—*that's* life."

The last of the black consumes the bones. The fire roars and crackles, flashing through reds and blues, until a shadow rises within, bones clicking together, fat bubbling and sizzling into place, muscles drawn taut, skin leavening over flesh.

A clatter of hoofbeats. The crack of a whip. A shout. Hàokōng and La Sombra turn to see Anselmo jumping off his horse and snarling with anger.

"It's done," La Sombra says.

"I told you to stop," Anselmo hisses, "after what happened to Papá."

Hot, furious tears run down Anselmo's cheeks. He turns, looming over Hàokōng, who says nothing. Words come to his tongue, but, in the face of Anselmo's fury, Hàokōng finds his lips unwilling to part.

"Do you know what you've created?" Anselmo says. "You've brought back the flesh and blood of the dead, but not their heart, nor their soul. Absent those, immortality simply grants the revenant license to destroy and abuse. They may wear the face of the one you love, but you'll witness them wreaking havoc that would devastate you to even think about. And you—"

He jabs a finger at Hàokōng's chest, right over his heart, words so furious that he spits them like a snake, all his friendliness gone.

"—*you* created that. *You* are responsible for this creature."

"Mijo," La Sombra says, giving Anselmo a sympathetic look, a somber smile touching the edges of her lips. "No one truly knows what will be created. Not this gentleman, nor me, nor you. You know as well as I do that every person has evil inside them. It was inside Octavio, and I told you, too, that it could show itself."

The fire dies down, leaving the blackened silhouette of a figure standing in the remains of the pyre. He's smaller than Hàokōng but still bears a striking resemblance to him, their features both high and flat, elegant and sharp. He opens his eyes, mirror images of Hàokōng's.

"Brother," he says, his voice raspy. The hairs on Hàokōng's arms and nape stand on end. The figure steps away from the pyre and turns to La Sombra, who gives him a weary look.

"Will you be the one who takes me?"

The figure grins.

"If only I could," he says, looking at La Sombra with the delight of a sadist in his eyes, something Hàokōng has never seen in his brother before.

La Sombra sighs and looks at her palm, her wrist, as if contemplating the pulsing veins underneath. She clenches her fingers as if she were wrapping them around marionette controls, then tightens them into a fist.

"It's a shame I'll never take my own life," she says.

"No," Anselmo says, holding his head high. "That isn't the shame, abuelita—that is courage. The shame is that you make the same choice over and over, expecting a different outcome each time."

La Sombra shakes her head.

"I know. And yet I keep thinking, maybe I will make up for Octavio someday and set things right, truly change someone's life for the better. But as for what happens now—" She looks up at Anselmo, her smile sad. "Go."

The figure advances on Hàokōng. He wants to embrace his brother, but even as his eyes well up with tears, he knows that this could never be Yìdié. The light is absent from his eyes, giving him the same sunken, hollow look as the man on the WANTED poster. The very air around him seems to warp and distort with dread. The expression on Yìdié's face is wicked and soulless, transforming him into a stranger. Hàokōng's heart sinks.

"Leave him," Anselmo says, grabbing Hàokōng by the wrist. "Leave your mule, too. Consider it payment. We'll be faster if we both ride my horse."

Hàokōng's skin crawls. His throat is too tight for words, his lungs compressed. He follows Anselmo, looking once over his shoulder as they hop on Anselmo's horse. Anselmo cracks his whip, and the horse breaks into a gallop, kicking up dust in their wake.

"Another one," Anselmo says as they ride back through the desert, the first sun creeping up over the horizon. Tears streak his face. "As if facing my father weren't enough."

Hàokōng's arms are wrapped tight around Anselmo's

waist, his face pressed against his pava-and-gunpowder-scented sarape. *I'm sorry*, Hàokōng wants to say, his fingertips gripping the fabric of Anselmo's shirt, ghosting over the muscle underneath, over Anselmo's firmness and strength—his solidity, the realness and sweat and salt that declare his presence.

Instead, all he manages is, "I thought it would work. I thought I could fix things."

The horse clatters past saguaros, past yucca palms, past squat cactuses and sprawling chaparral. The last of the night blossoms wither away as the suns rise higher, illuminating the wavering image of Agua Oscuro on the horizon.

To Hàokōng's surprise, Anselmo barks out a laugh, low and dark. His face twists into a humorless grin, his voice heavy, the words hovering only a moment before the wind whips them away.

"We all do."

～

Vessel speaks as se places the marionette back in its cubby. "Are you troubled?"

Se turns back around to face Anima, the hem of ser dress twirling like the curls of ser hair: slow, elegant whirlpools of darkness.

"Why do you ask?" Anima replies.

"You're clenching your fists."

Anima looks down. Indeed æ is. Æ opens ær hands, taking in the crescents pitted into the flesh of ær palms. It takes a moment for ær to realize that ær tension comes not from unease but from indignation, hot under ær breastbone, ready to burst.

"Life and death are a natural cycle," Anima says.

Vessel regards Anima for a moment, amused, as if se's withholding the punchline to a joke.

"We can still have power over natural things, no?" Se touches ser index finger to ser cheek, inquisitive. "Haven't you, too, determined whether a person will live or die?"

Anima's stem pulses. Images of the fugitive flash through ær mind. Suppose æ had caught him; suppose æ had turned him in to the authorities. For what crime—crossing a border in pursuit of a human connection?

Pain knifes through Anima's skull. Æ leans forward, elbows digging into ær thighs, thumbs pressing against ær temples. Even though æ feels as if æ's sinking into a pit, the chair does not sway, nor does the liana creak. Ær vision flickers, going black before swimming back into focus.

One shaky breath, then another. Anima swallows, wetting ær lips and tongue. When æ looks up again, Vessel is still looking at ær, as if observing a specimen under glass. Æ steps out of the bubble chair, ær toes flushing as æ stands, and gestures with a shaking hand. The chair comes undone, twisting out into vines again that retreat to wrap around the trunk of the great, hanging tree.

"I need a moment alone," Anima says.

"You must offer something precious of yours to the qíjìtáng," Vessel replies, voice honey-warm and smooth. "Shall I return at a later time to collect it?"

"Please," Anima says. Æ does not wait for Vessel to say anything more. Anima turns away from Vessel, stem arching high behind ær, tethered to the world tree like a ribbon, giving ær room to walk back to ær pod.

Æ does not look back as æ closes the fronds around ær and sinks into the bath.

Anima borrows the body of a night raven doing its rounds. Unlike the solid-bodied birds found in other parts of Aurei, the night raven is as immaterial as an aurora. Instead of being powered by physics and machinery like the day crow, the night raven draws its power from the concentrated pava circulating through its system.

Anima prefers the day crow, if only because it is a more

predictable system. The night raven is, by its nature, un-predictable: pava affects everyone differently. Its thera-peutic dosage is so individual that finding the optimal level for anyone is a science in itself, one that Anima prefers not to dabble in. Too many unknown variables.

Anima soars high above the city. The transparent body of the night raven shimmers with stars captured within its borders. There, invisible against the spangled sky, An-ima observes the Hub. It is the pride of Ora, the heart that powers the entire city. The rough trunk of the great tree pierces through the ground; not far from Anima's motionless human body is part of the tree's crown, to which Anima's stem is directly connected. Like a mirror image of the crown, the roots of the Hub extend toward the sky, anchoring themselves to other trees and to the biometal canopy walkways, where the Gleaming leaks through the finer, capillary-like mycorrhizal networks that interface with the roots, infusing the entire city with the planet's qì.

The ability to body hop is what distinguishes the in-ner sanctum nodes like Anima from the others. Any node—the binary ones with two people, the trinary ones with three, even the tetrary ones with four per chamber—can fold the Gleaming to look out from the eyes of another being infused with its energy. But only the innermost eight nodes have developed the ability to borrow a body and control it. Hopping into a person's head is still impossible, to say nothing of the ethics of such a trespass, but for all other creatures, the Gleaming transforms Anima's presence into another cortical layer that wraps around the animal's brain, giving Anima control over its perceptions and movements. Even so, the lizard brain underneath still powers the creature's responses and the way it perceives the world.

The pava concentrate that powers both the day crow and the night raven enhances the artificial creatures' receptiveness to the Gleaming, just as the pava concentrate in Anima's stem enhances ær own cerebral processing capabilities, allowing ær to form a network with other nodes to simultaneously process increasingly more complex data. Although ær powers are mostly limited to the city, despite the Gleaming's theoretical connection to everywhere else on the planet, Anima finds monitoring just the city to be a hefty enough task in itself.

The city always evolves. But the Gleaming does not—there is nothing for it to evolve *from*.

Anima releases the night raven. Æ drifts back into ær human body, limited and anchored to a chamber from which æ can never leave—at least, not physically.

Æ closes ær eyes. Lets ær head dip under the amniotic fluid, lets ær limbs, ær belly, ær knees be submerged, until there is nothing left above the surface but ær nostrils and lips. Æ floats, dreamlike, and lets ær senses fade away to nothingness. Then, with a breath, æ relaxes ær stem, falls into the Gleaming, and melts into the steady pulse of golden light.

Anima unfocuses ær still-closed eyes and lets ær inner gaze come together in the center of ær forehead to look out into the Gleaming. There is only one sense here: the sixth. For several breaths, æ lets ær body hang motionless as motes and crystals of light stream around ær. Here, the backdrop to the Gleaming is the blooming viridian of the cloud forest covering Ora. In the Skylands, the Convergence is snowy white; in some parts of Samiyo, the Manifold is the darkened vermilion of sandstone bluffs, while in others, the Elegance the rich azure of the deepest sea. The light, however, remains gold throughout the world.

After ær breathing has evened out, once ær heartbeat has crescendoed to pound against ær eardrums, Anima touches one hand to ær belly, traces it down the midline that leads to ær navel, and rests it there for several more breaths. Ær belly swells like a wave, then deflates to a basin. Æ releases the tension in ær sacrum, longing for a tail to lift as æ tilts ær hips, parts ær legs.

Time does not exist in the Gleaming. It is an eternal moment, infinitesimally small slices of the present integrating into the calculus of being. There is no past or future, only now, only breath and blood, bone and sinew, muscle and neuron. The Gleaming is a sea in the mind; the Gleaming is a collective dream; the Gleaming is the space within, bigger than ær body could ever contain.

Still, there is something cathartic about having a body through which energy can be vented. An exit for the riot of emotions coursing through ær. When æ drops ær hand to between ær legs, touches ær fingertips to the flushed, tender flesh there, a sense of majesty shudders through ær, as if æ is a god touching a universe, sparking life through the landscape.

Anima has seen sex in all configurations of bodies, all permutations of partners. But æ does not call up those scenes as ær fingertips dance over ær quivering skin. Should ær mind wander, conjuring images of the world outside the Gleaming, Anima focuses once again on ær breathing: inhale, exhale, over and over. Grazes ær nails over ær skin, trailing goose bumps, circles ær other hand around ær threshold, lighting ærself with desire, coiled, simmering.

Entering ærself is to enter a world within a world. Æ has no physical body in the Gleaming—only sensation, only presence. In the Gleaming, æ is not the body but the walls, the limits of the universe within. Entering ærself is to spark a supernova, bright and building, perceptible only after the explosion has already begun.

The Gleaming is everywhere, and it is nowhere. It is

simultaneous. It intersects with itself. All beings are infused with the power of it, yet only a few can access it directly. Even if Anima can sense the presence of others within the Gleaming, æ cannot perceive them, not within the Gleaming itself. To interact through the Gleaming as æ did with Enigma requires a body, even if it is animal; there need to be discrete ends for communication to occur.

But, detached from ær body with no other anchor, Anima is simply a stratum in the Gleaming, existing within it like everyone else: a plane in a shared dimension. The Gleaming is one, even as it is none.

Anima strokes ærself, gasps as a field of wildflowers bursts into bloom, as a pelican guzzles down a fish, its beak an open maw, its throat distended. With ær other hand, æ presses deeper into ærself. A fire starts deep in ær gut, full and warm, chasing through ær abdomen to the peaks of each nipple. Æ quakes, lips trembling, full of honeybee-lightning buzz, as if heralding an oncoming storm.

When Anima brushes against the spot that unravels ær, it is as if æ is a seed about to germinate, there on the cusp of that border. Æ is a flash flood rushing to obliterate everything in its path. Snakes tangled together, writhing; a murmuration of birds, a sleek school of fish that breaks, scatters to let the light of the surface through, becomes the seafoam limning an ocean wave glittering with moonlight as it crashes onto the shore, cascades like a stampede of white horses advancing over a desert. Æ pulses like a jellyfish, contracts, leaves tendrils of pleasure in ær wake, stinging embers, the remnants of a blackened forest, ready to grow anew.

Æ lingers in the stillness, listening as ær heartbeat dampens to a more muted frequency. Ær fingerprints are bloated, water wrinkling the landscape into peaks and valleys furrowed with soaked lichen.

Anima returns to ær body. Opens ær eyes, greets the veined ceiling of ær node once more. It is always a disappointment to remember that æ is limited by the confines of ær physical body, and that it is only the stem that gives ær such direct access to the Gleaming. Without it, what would æ be? Another human, indistinguishable from any other; a human who can see only through ær own eyes and never another's.

It's not as if æ's never been that.

Æ has simply spent so long as a node that æ has forgotten how it feels to live otherwise.

———————

Ær task today is to filter through financial data in search of evidence of fraud. The treasury suspects that there is a money laundering operation in the city. The task is less exciting than chasing after a fugitive, but such commotion is rare. The daily work of a node is much of this: using the superhumanity bestowed by the direct connection to the Gleaming to process tasks at a much faster speed than any one person can handle. As one of the eight nodes in the inner sanctum, Anima is quick and experienced. Æ sifts through parcels of data, pulses them back through the Hub, then sifts through more data, ær third eye open to spot inconsistencies in complicated patterns.

Still, going through endless data takes its toll, even on an enhanced mind and body. Anima steps out of the pod for a break. Even if the amniotic bath keeps ær muscles from atrophying, it feels good to use them anyway, if only for the sensory stimulation of ær muscles and tendons stretching.

Æ balances ærself on one foot, palms pressed together before ær chest, arch of the other foot pressed to ær inner thigh. Æ used to only be able to press ær foot to ær calf, but the more æ observes ær body as a machine—an organic machine, not one of biometal—the more æ connects to the mechanics of it, the intricate details and calibrations. Before, æ had only considered the force of pulling: shying away, making distance. Now, æ experiments with pushing, finding the solidity of force and weight counterbalancing one another, stability in itself.

Anima shifts to ær other foot, mirroring the tree pose. Frustrating, how æ is not a perfect gyroscope that remains level. Ær right side is tighter than ær left. Variation in balance; a natural configuration, like handedness. But, as æ lands heavily on the ball of ær foot again, æ can't help but feel annoyed.

It is then that Vessel strolls in again with the qíjìtáng. Anima is trained to speak calmly and to not let emotions interfere, but irritation creeps into ær voice as æ turns to address Vessel.

"How did you get into the Hub?" Anima asks.

"Nothing escapes your notice, does it?" Vessel says, amused. "Even among people watching everything, you're sharper than most."

Today, Vessel wears a brilliant, emerald-green dress laced through with gold, the hem stopping just above the knees, the sleeves ending in gentle lobes of glittering embroidery. Se has a butterfly pin in ser hair; ser eyes are lined dark with kohl. The snake hovers over ser shoulders like a ribbon.

"I didn't question you before," Anima says, "but I ask you now—which authority granted you permission to enter the Hub?"

"Authority?" Vessel says, smiling.

"Yes," Anima says, firmly, even as doubt begins to take

root. "Whose business are you here on?"

"No one's," se says.

"You need permission to enter the Hub," Anima says, pressing on. "I have found no record of your entry. You must realize that infiltration is a grave offense in Ora."

Anima hesitates, eyes flitting over the closed qíjitáng. The memory of the marionette, the story within—still, æ has a duty to at least inform Vessel of the consequences. The city has built itself on shared laws and governance. The few outsiders who visit are not exempt from knowing the code of conduct. Ora is a safe haven because of that shared contract, and Anima is a part of ensuring that contract is enforced.

"Infiltrators are sentenced to death," Anima says at last.

For a moment, Vessel's facade slips, revealing something deeply human in ser dark eyes. But, as Anima speaks again, Vessel recovers, the walls smoothly back in place.

"You must understand that Ora is a city-state in exile," Anima continues. "We have suffered enormous collective trauma. And so, we must guarantee our citizens' safety. Everyone must be known. The punishment for lying is far worse than that for telling the truth."

Vessel sighs.

"I suppose I have no choice, then," se says, smiling ruefully. "I'm a psychopomp. Not quite alive, not quite dead.

I travel through the orthogonal plane to get places. So I can bypass your gates and security easily."

Anima isn't sure how to take the information. There is lore about psychopomps existing in other cultures, and æ is vaguely aware of the orthogonal plane, but æ thought it was a theological construct. Æ picks at the tangle of thoughts, then settles on the first response that seems safe.

"That's a major security flaw," æ says. "Especially if you can take others with you through the plane."

To ær surprise, Vessel laughs, teeth bright, apples of ser cheeks high, corners of ser eyes wrinkling.

"You're different," is all Vessel says in response, puzzling Anima. "I was expecting questions, at least."

"Oh," Anima says, feeling suddenly embarrassed. "Well then, first of all—*can* you take people with you through the plane?"

"Yes. But I don't," Vessel says, shrugging. "I work solo."

"All right." Anima pauses, then continues with ær next question: "Who are you, really?"

"Let's just say that I was supposed to die, but I didn't," Vessel answers. "I've got some things to take care of, and then I can get out of limbo and take another shot at life."

"What things?"

"Stories," Vessel says, unlatching the qíjìtáng. As it unfolds, ser words punctuate the clatters and snaps. "Histories. Lives. It's my job to collect them until this qíjìtáng is full."

Neither Anima nor Vessel speaks as the qíjìtáng springs into shape. Anima sweeps ær eyes over the shelves. It seems as if each nook, each shelf, each hollow, each drawer contains something. There is only a single shelf in the center that is empty. The last carved screens slide out into place.

"So you're almost done," Anima says. Vessel nods.

"Just one more specimen."

"Mine," Anima says, looking over to Vessel, whose smile is less mysterious now—more human, more full of wants and needs.

"Yes. But I can't just take it from you. You have to offer it to me."

What can æ offer? A frond from ær node? No; that seems so trivial, so replaceable compared to the marionette and the other items æ doesn't even have names for. All æ knows is that they are precious.

"I don't have much to my name," Anima says. "I don't have stories of faraway places like you do. I've only ever lived in Ora."

"You might not have a great quantity of stories," Vessel says, "but you will always have at least one: the story of your life."

Æ laughs at the very idea.

"My life? What could possibly be interesting about it?" Æ gestures at the walls around the two of them. "I'm always here."

"I said a story, not a set of coordinates," Vessel says, eyes twinkling. "There is something that remains *you* no matter where you are, when you are, what you are. So, I'll ask you one question: Who are you?"

"I'm—" Anima begins, then finds ærself stalling already. Should æ provide ær terminal name, Anima, or ær birth name? Here in the Hub, Anima only ever uses ær terminal name. In fact, æ has gone by "Anima" for longer than æ ever used ær birth name. Does ær terminal name apply only to the Anima that exists after becoming a node, or does the name encompass even the world before that transition?

Vessel doesn't press Anima to answer quickly.

"It might be a long story," Anima admits, still caught up in where to even begin.

"Please," Vessel says, nodding respectfully, "it would be my honor to listen."

Anima takes a deep breath. In ær mind's eye, æ sees ærself in different times, across different places. With an exhale, Anima begins to speak.

~

0.

i can trace myself back to skylander ancestors:
   insurgents who ended the empire
     that was projecting its shadow
       onto the world

   fighters / dreamers / scholars
     who were disappeared
       one / after / another
by the hand of a new empire
     calling itself
       a federated democracy.

i can trace myself back to my birth
   if that is where i begin—

     —but am i not already in
       the stars—the leaves—the air—
         —the Gleaming that permeates us all?

did i not already exist in my parents
   in the soil of my nation
   in what my blood has already known
     before it filled my body?

i am not me without my heritage.

my story began
long before i did.

1.

my father was a kitsune
     my mother was a human.

we lived in a small apartment
     over the storefront
          where my father told fortunes.

back then i was named
     morishima shadarev.
               i went to school like other children
                    saved my spare change like they did
                         for candied apricots and shaved ice

                    but for all the sweetness on my tongue
                         i knew i was not
                              truly like them.

i averted my gaze
     even as i sought patterns

in people's behavior:

      perhaps then i could discover
        the rules of engagement,
          a logic
            i could program
        into myself.

my mother

  (slender-faced
     golden-skinned
       eyes night-dark)

        pours chicken stock over bulgur
          sets the bones aside to be ground

        cracks eggs into a bowl
          whisks them with chopsticks
        cascades them into the pan
        to sizzle with the meat

    my father
seated downstairs
    scries each face that enters
      to excavate its history

its desires / its fears
the places where worry
knots the skin
and transforms into the image
each client most wants to see

(people always assumed
my mother was the fortune-teller.

(but even though she broke apart bones
(pounded them (in (the mortar (with (the pestle
(until (the meal (was fine (as flour

she was not the one)
who read the stories)
in their marrow.)

some nights
my father needed only to tell the truth
but more often than not
he had to bend the truth
even if it pained him
knowing that he could not prevent
the tragedies written in the future

for he always thought of us upstairs:

my mother blanketing a bed of bulgur
    with steaming chicken and eggs
as i set the table in anticipation
      of my father's return.

he thinks about how much it costs
    to put food on the table
    a roof over our heads
    clothes on our backs.

much as he loathed telling lies and half-truths
my father could not refuse his clients' requests.

once he'd spun enough stories for the night
my father would return upstairs
    transforming with each step
      from whatever form he had taken
    whether that was
        a young woman dressed neatly in a yukata
        or an older woman dressed
          in an opulent kimono

when he sits down across from me
the person on the other side of the dinner table
    is just a man
      who looks like any other uncle

his white shirt pulled up over his potbelly
his long hair pulled back into a bun
as messy as his beard is scruffy

a man
who once told me
as if to console me
when i asked why i couldn't transform like him,
why i had only one form
even though i felt many inside,

"you don't need to be a kitsune
to be someone else. that's
the easy part,"

he'd said,
taking my hand
turning the palm toward the sky
so he could trace
my lifeline.

"what's harder
is being yourself so completely
that there is still a 'you'
no matter the form you hold."

2.

every child in ora knows that there is a world
beyond the borders of the city.

     every child in ora knows
there is nothing to want from that world.
   after all,
     we are provided with all we ever need
      all we could ever want.

we have the longest life spans of any nation
   the highest literacy rates
     the best education
    the best healthcare—
  choose any measure
  and i can tell you
how we surpass the rest of the world in it.

        what of the unmeasurable?

there is nothing
that cannot be quantified,
  cannot be surpassed,
  cannot be
    exploited.

3.

you can leave the city—
                    —if you have reason to.

my mother

  (a courier
      bearing messages on paper
        for the rest of the world to read)

      shows her exit visa
    at every io gate
          told me when i asked through tears
              why i couldn't go with her
          why she was gone
              for weeks at a time,

                        "the rest of the world
                        must never forget
                        that we are still here."

my mother
    ferrying messages to outside shores
  wished for another life
          never told me her desires

her stories
who she was
never asked me if i too
wanted to leave

"it's safer here,"

she would say
as if in explanation.

"you will be provided for here.
you will not want for anything here."

i never had the chance to ask
then why don't you want to stay?

4.

my father
could not tell his own fortune
did not see how bending other people's truths
transmuting their pain
into palatable narratives
knowing he could never intervene
would imprint shadows
onto him too

some nights
the weight of other people's futures
would drive my father to shroud himself in pava
smoke
as he looked out into
an unseen expanse

) in my mother's absence (

my father
had no one but me
to hear his pain.

(it was only later i learned
a child is not meant
to be made secretkeeper
to guard a parent's emotions
at the expense of their own.)

my mother
tells my father
there are other ways to make a living
that will not cause him
so much pain

tells him

there are others like you
in liola / goren / bethana
kitsune who live as they are
who don't have to register every one of their
faces
who can simply be

all you have to do
is cross an ocean.

5.

i was nine
when my parents left.
my father wore someone else's face
as he showed a stolen exit visa
at the io gate.

my mother had told me
they would only be gone for a few weeks
just enough time to prepare a new home
where we would be happier.

by then
my mother's absences
had already worn familiar grooves

into my aching
        unmoored
           bones.

kept in the care
of grandparents
   aunts   uncles
      weeks   became months

   i pored over absence
buried my face in the jacket my mother left behind
   sobbing for her return
      even as i knew my tears
      would wash away
   what little perfume still lingered

stole bones from my father's apothecary catalog
        stoked fires / laid down the blades
      waited for the marrow to bubble
      waited for it to tell me *what*
          i wanted to know   *where*
              / *when*
           Why

   but even as i begged the universe
   to tell me its logic

to make some kind of sense
out of the turmoil inside me

the bones
    /
kept their silence.

my father's eldest sister
pulled me away from the flames
    steadied me / wiped my tears
        told me gently,

            "your mother and father
                are not coming back."

i didn't yet know
what citizenship was
    why revoking it meant
i could no longer see my parents
    didn't yet understand
what a border was
    why crossing one
        didn't always mean
            you could return

set adrift

i withdrew
severed everything myself
before it could be severed

left school when i was eleven
to join the Hub
where i was given my terminal name—

Anima

—alongside the only other recruit my age

Enigma.

now
i have roots
now
my sight extends to the sky
now
i am no longer ever
alone.

~

When Anima finishes speaking, æ is weightless, hands
buzzing, cold with sweat. It is the first time æ has ever

spoken about ærself so extensively. A story that seems mundane to ær, yet it feels as if the schism within ær has widened, as if it has inhaled, diaphragm tensed before the eventual exhale.

The exhalation comes as a pulse through the Gleaming, a flash as a surge of motes and light leaves through ær stem. The flash illuminates the room for only a half second, but in that light, Anima sees Vessel's intrigue.

"How fascinating this city is," se says. "So unlike my own."

Anima tilts ær head.

"And where are you from?"

"Nameron," se replies. "On the mainland of Samiyo, where the Delicia River empties into the sea."

"The mainland," Anima echoes, imagining a land so expansive that it is impossible to travel across it like you could across Ora in a day. A continent so large that a journey across it on foot is a death wish. "What is that like—living somewhere that isn't an island?"

"Well, first of all, it's too big for any one person to say what all of it is like," Vessel says, amused. "And besides, I can only really tell you what Nameron is like, and even then, only the part of it that I've experienced. Alas, I'm not omnipresent the way you are."

Omnipresent. Anima considers the word. True for some value—æ can be anywhere in the city at any time—but also completely incorrect—Anima can only truly be in one place, one body at a time, and when æ is in the Gleaming, æ is not "present" at all.

Still, Anima does not interrupt Vessel to correct ser on the nuances.

"It's a city much the opposite of this one, even if it's exactly the same in other ways. Where yours is built from trauma, mine is built on hope. Nameron is the new capital of the Mugrosan Lowlands. It is meant to be a harmonious rebirth from the conflict that has characterized northern Samiyo. A city where each citizen is afforded equality and the same opportunity to realize their potential."

Se gives a wry smile.

"Of course, you can imagine that such pressure to achieve and climb can backfire. And often, you cannot see such burnout until after it has happened."

"I don't know if I can imagine that. In Ora, we work in service of all other citizens. We each have a path and a place in society."

"How pleasant," Vessel says, then chuckles. "And utterly terrifying."

"Terrifying?" Anima says, cocking ær head. "How?"

Vessel shakes ser head.

"Maybe you'll understand with time. Or maybe I'm the one who's mistaken."

Se waves a hand at the qíjìtáng, the arc of ser wrist like

a waterfall. The qíjìtáng folds in on itself, clattering and creaking, until it is once more an octagonal trunk.

"I will still need something from you," se says. "But for now, I must depart. I will return soon."

Se bows and takes ser leave. Even after the hallways have fallen silent, Anima continues to stare at the moon gate.

————————

As a node, Anima does not need to eat or drink. Æ has never been one to luxuriate in food anyway. It was a relief to have that need excised. Food and drink to ær have always been reminders that ær body is, in the end, organic, and relies on the same processes as any other animal. Nourishment was never more than a chore. Many other nodes prefer to still eat out of some kind of psychological need, but Anima is happy to give up food and drink if it means æ can sink into a flow state for hours at a time, focus uninterrupted, not even by ær own body.

Nonetheless, æ still has some curiosity about food, and consuming it in an animal's body makes the experience more dignified, as if it's somehow more natural. As if the existential crisis of fending off death with every meal has lifted, replaced only with instinctual drives. Eating becomes entertainment, a voyeuristic look through another being's eyes. So, when Anima tires of processing data, æ disengages from the Gleaming and drops into the body of a wild dog.

The dog is the easiest to maneuver on ær trips to the market. Rats, mice, and wasps also have excellent senses of smell, but they are far less welcome. Dogs still get shooed away, but if æ picks one that isn't too scruffy, æ gets the occasional smile and scrap of food.

The outdoor market gathers from forthlight to suns risen, before the day gets too hot, so that the produce stays fresh and the ice doesn't melt too quickly. Past that, the outdoor bazaar closes shop and gives way to the indoor wet market, which runs until both suns have set. Then, the night market opens up outdoors, with vendors selling food, drink, gifts, clothing—all manner of items for purchase.

Anima likes the night market best. Not just because people pay less mind to the wild animals sharing the city with them, but also because it is such a sensory riot. Like a single meal for a snake, one night at the market leaves Anima satiated so that the sameness of ær hall becomes a relief. Like meditation, compared to the excess of the outside world.

The dog Anima is borrowing tonight is a handsome mutt, coat white and gray and black. As æ steps out of the alley onto Anatoma Street, the full majesty of the night market hits ær. Paper lanterns strung up over woven eaves, clouds of steam and smoke drifting like fog, scents settling on the oils of ær fur like dew. Chatter in multiple languages; sizzling; the scrape of metal on metal; the sharp *clink!* of glasses coming together in a toast. The air is thicker here, as if a magical quality has suffused it, turning a street that is ordinary by day into something otherworldly by night. Even the light comes in a dozen colors: the cool blue-white of the moon; the twinkling, honey-amber string lights; the rainbows diffusing through thin lanterns of blue and red and yellow paper; the fluttering of the orange flames in the gas lamps lining the sidewalk.

Anima follows the buffet of smells. Fresh strawberries topping shaved ice. Batter pouring into cake molds. Rich soup stock, rendered for days. Eventually, Anima wanders over to one stall in particular, where a veritable pike skewers an abominably large pile of meat. The rotisserie turns, giving the pillar of meat a beautiful golden char. Every now and then, a man slices off some of the meat and layers it with bright vegetables on thin bread.

If Anima whines at the right passerby, perhaps æ can get some scraps and feel the dog's sharp teeth clamp down on the meat and shred it to pieces. But even as a dog, æ has little appreciation for flavor beyond distinguishing what kind of meat æ's eating.

Anima is scanning the crowd for someone who can help with ær scheme when æ notices a familiar figure.

Vessel.

Se's sitting alone at a table on the patio of a late-night café, a modest cup of coffee and a small plate with a delicate pastry before ser. The snake cascades down ser shoulders, then ser forearm, and slithers onto the table, where it coils into a pile.

"I don't know why you wassste your money on thingsss you can't even enjoy," it hisses. Anima's hackles rise as æ pads closer and disappears into a shadow in the alley by the coffee shop. Animals have spoken in legend, and the Skylanders have long kept talking birds, but this is the first time Anima has seen an animal speak ærself.

"Because it makes me feel normal," Vessel snaps.

The snake laughs.

"'Normal' isss an illusssion. You will die chasssing it. You have more worthwhile tasssksss to invessst your time in," the snake says, giving Vessel a pointed look. The pastry, untouched on the plate, is tempting—under Anima's cortex, the dog's brain lights up in recognition of sugar. But, although no one but the nodes has ever been able to distinguish a borrowed animal from one that isn't, Anima doesn't want to risk it with Vessel—æ has no idea how ser perception differs from others, whether, somehow, se would recognize ær.

Æ settles into the shadows and continues to eavesdrop.

"Don't tell me you're having doubtsss now," the snake says, undulating to sit up, tall, black scales shimmering iridescently like an oil slick.

"Of course I am. This is the last memento I need. After this . . ."

"You get a sssecond shot at life."

"I don't want one."

"Nonsssenssse," the snake says, flicking its tongue out with irritation. "You became a psssychopomp becaussse you begged for one."

"That was before I knew what being one meant," Vessel retorts.

"Don't you want to live your own life again insssstead of collecting othersss'?" the snake says. "Don't you want to eat and drink again? To sssleep again?"

"I don't think I do," Vessel says, pushing the pastry away. "I was never as happy alive as I am now. I've got a purpose here. There's always another story to find. Always. You never need to talk to anyone long to find something touched by the soul."

"Ssso what are you going to do, then?" the snake says. "Leave the qíjìtáng incomplete and fade away to utter nonexisssstenccce?"

"I know I don't want that, at least. Maybe there's something I can do after the rebirth. I don't know." Se smiles ruefully. Picks up the cup and saucer, brings them to ser lips, blows on the coffee to cool it. Puts everything down again. "At least I'll still have all my memories. I won't make the same mistakes again."

"Maybe it'sss time to ssstop letting the outssside in and ssstart letting out what isss within," the snake says, nodding, tongue tasting the air.

"What's that supposed to mean?"

"Jussst a sssuggessstion."

The snake winds back up Vessel's arm to rest again on ser shoulders. As Vessel stands, the snake rocks, then ripples to hover in the air, floating around Vessel's ears. Just as Anima stands to follow them, Vessel and the snake disappear.

Anima releases the dog, all thoughts of eating gone once more. When æ opens ær eyes in the node, pushes apart the fronds, and steps out, Vessel is already waiting for ær with the qíjìtáng open.

"I was hoping to beat you back here," se says, smiling. Anima flushes, ready to respond, but Vessel waves away ær concerns. "I trade on curiosity and could never fault you for it. Now, do you have anything for me?"

Anima shakes ær head.

"I'm afraid not."

"That's all right," Vessel says. "After all, your contribution allows you to browse the whole collection. I, too, would not be satisfied if I told you about only one of the mementos."

Vessel steps aside, hands clasped before ser.

"Go ahead. Pick out another item. I would be happy to tell you more about it."

In some ways, the qíjìtáng is even more overwhelming than the night market, even if it is meticulously organized. Anima spares ærself the exhaustion of browsing and selects the first thing that catches ær eye—an ornate bowl with a spike under it.

"Oh, the skycup is a good choice," Vessel says. "Do you like playing sports, Anima?"

Æ thinks back to recreation periods in school: fumbling through games and hating all exercise until æ realized that æ simply had to be active solo.

"Can't say I do."

"Then maybe this will change your mind," Vessel says. Se sets the top on its point and spins it with a flick of ser wrist. As the skycup comes to an impossibly perfect equilibrium, its spirit and history unfold together.

~

S. Qiouyi Lu

This Form I Hold Now

Fistfights break out among the spectators. The staff attempts to pacify the crowd, but the shouting only amplifies to a furious roar. People spill out of their seats and rush the ring, where guards surround the judges, referee, and scorekeeper.

"This does not look good," Chūnjú says weakly.

———

On her third birthday, Chūnjú announces that she's a girl.

Her parents don't ask her if she's sure. It's useless to ask any three-year-old if they're sure of anything. Nor do they tell Chūnjú that she's mistaken.

But when Chūnjú is six, she announces to her mother that she wants to bind her feet.

"You don't have to," her mother says. Her own feet are silver lotuses, not the tiniest golden lotuses, but still delicate and only a few inches long. She totters when she walks, her movements unsteady, as if her refined clothes and jewelry leave her unbalanced.

Chūnjú's father smiles when he sees her mother walk. And all the aunties who come to visit have bound feet, too, though not nearly as small as her mother's.

"I want to."

Chūnjú's mother stands at the kitchen counter preparing fruit. A palm-size, golden melon shines in the late-afternoon sunlight. She peels the skin, then cuts the melon into crisp pieces, their sugar-sweet scent hanging in the air as she steps over to the kitchen table and sets down the porcelain plate of sliced melon.

But rather than enjoying the fruit together with their usual jokes and smiles, Chūnjú watches as her mother remains silent, her gaze distant.

"Mămá?"

Chūnjú's mother looks into her daughter's imploring eyes. She sets down her slice of melon.

"Jújú, do you know how they make feet so small?"

Chūnjú nods, her ponytail bobbing. "They bend your toes and push really hard."

Chūnjú's mother's lips curve into a half smile. "Yes, Jújú. And when they bend your toes, they bend them so hard, they break." She pauses. "It hurts a lot, darling."

But if anything, Chūnjú's gaze only becomes more resolute, even as a little wavering fear comes through. Chūnjú spears a slice of melon on one chopstick—"Jújú, please, have some manners"—and munches on it energetically. Her mother can't help but laugh.

"I'm not afraid!" she says. "I want to be the fifth beauty of the Empire!" She does bear a resemblance to the courtesans who make up the Four Beauties—their slender faces and dewy skin, eyes gleaming with rich depths that show an inner brilliance.

But that is now, when she is six years old and more or less unisex. Chūnjú's mother bites her lip for a moment, mulling over how to phrase her thoughts.

"Chūnjú."

She looks up—if her mother is using her actual name, she needs to pay attention.

"You don't have to be a girl."

Chūnjú makes a puzzled expression. "What do you mean?"

"In time, when you become an adult, your body will change in ways you won't expect." Chūnjú's mother hesitates. When she speaks once more, Chūnjú senses the boiling turbulence of fear and resentment and anger modulating her words: "You will also give up many things. You will play less and spend more time at home doing women's work. People will look at you differently. You give up the easy way to take the hard way."

Chūnjú furrows her brow, like she understands the words her mother is saying but not what they mean together.

"What I'm saying is," her mother continues, "if you were to decide not to be a girl anymore, you can grow up to look like boys, and you will have an easier life."

Chūnjú frowns. "But boys don't bind their feet."

"That's right. And it saves them pain and gives them more freedom to work and live in comfort."

"But *we* live in comfort."

Chūnjú's mother smiles.

"I'm glad you think so. But it takes work to make life comfortable. Life is already hard enough. You don't need to add more pain."

She pulls Chūnjú close. Chūnjú's baby feet are bare against the wooden floor, her toes flexed like a gecko's to grip the ground and bear her weight as she stands steady, head to her mother's chest.

But Chūnjú hasn't changed her mind by her next birthday. So Táo Āyí steps in to supervise the process. A mother never oversees her own daughter's foot-binding—she may pity the girl and not pull her bindings as tightly, so as to spare her pain.

Binding is easier in the winter, when there is ice to numb her feet. It is best to bind a foot before it has fully developed. The sooner she can start, the better.

Chūnjú is ready. At least, she thinks she is. Still, she's shocked by the steaming basins of dark animal blood and pungent herbs filling the air with the scent of medicine and the apothecary. She squirms as she waits for Táo Āyí to finish the preparations.

Táo Āyí hobbles over to Chūnjú. She's somewhere in her sixties, her face only lined when she smiles. Her own feet are also silver lotuses, though they are closer to gold than Chūnjú's mother's. The occasional girl who achieves golden feet gets whisked away for marriage or to serve a noble. Chūnjú has never seen one around Kartang.

"Breathe," Táo Āyí says as she massages Chūnjú's right foot first, the bones pliant beneath her strong fingertips. "This will be over sooner than you expect."

She bends back Chūnjú's toes. And bends. And bends, until they break with an awful, symphonized crunch, and Chūnjú screams, passing out from the pain.

When she comes to, her feet still throb and burn, but they are now wrapped up in red-and-white bandages and ribbons.

Chūnjú smiles.

"Representing Liola . . . Sūn Chūnjú, from Kartang!"

Chūnjú had no idea the arena would be as packed as it is. Combat skycups is a fairly new sport, derived from the solo dance performances that brought the sport to the eye of the general public from the Tiānkyo elite. Even if the sport has an association with their floating colonizers, nationalism doesn't turn people away. If anything, combat skycups is a venue to *express* nationalism. Besides, the Calebriad Games haven't been held in forty years. It's not surprising that people are turning out in record numbers. And this year's games are being held in New Ologundu, just to the southeast across the strait and the bay from Kartang, easily accessible from multiple regions.

"And representing Goren ... Siya Chandrabayan, of Tali!"

Her opponent has dark skin and wavy black hair cropped short on the sides, the top an abundance of curls and waves that remind Chūnjú of the deep, turbulent Hǎilèi Sea. They have on a gender-neutral variant of the Gorenese sarong, similar to what some people wear in Kartang, even if Chūnjú herself is dressed in the breezy, fluttering sleeves and pants more typical of her own people. Chūnjú's outfit is sky blue with gold highlights that match the brass of the pneumatic braces supporting her bound feet. She was the first to use an assistive device in the Calebriads, and she had to demonstrate to a committee how she could both calibrate the pneumatics and ensure that she could keep them at a level that wouldn't create an unfair advantage over her opponents. Satisfied that Chūnjú would commit to good sportsmanship, the committee trained referees on how to inspect her braces as part of the routine equipment check before every match.

The referee gestures for the contestants to approach the center of the ring, where six skycups are laid out bowl-down in two rows: small, medium, and large. Chūnjú and Siya step up almost in sync, though Chūnjú's gait is more balanced compared to Siya's masculine swagger. Chūnjú can't tell if the swagger is for show or for real. She meets Siya's eyes as they size each other up. The referee inspects the wands, threads, and skycups, then Chūnjú's braces.

"All clear! Bow," the referee commands. Chūnjú and Siya comply, bending at the waist to acknowledge each other, both of them with one fist against the other palm as a sign of respect.

"Set!" the referee calls. Chūnjú and Siya take three skycups each and wind them onto the threads. Chūnjú falls into the familiar motion of tugging and releasing the wands to rev all three skycups to speed.

"Round one, go!"

Chūnjú leaps back to give herself more space, keeping her skycups in rotation close to her body. Her legs end up exposed as she guards her torso, but a hit to either of them will only score one point to the torso's two.

Siya, meanwhile, immediately idles the medium and large skycups, spinning them on the ground behind them as they get the smallest skycup to speed. To Chūnjú's surprise, Siya tosses the skycup high into the air, leaving their chest open. Instinct takes over as Chūnjú flings her large skycup down to idle it. The bowl wobbles but finds its equilibrium. Siya whips their thread out parallel to the ground. Chūnjú doesn't have time to set the other sky-cups down before Siya's thread whips around to catch the falling skycup and hurl it toward Chūnjú.

Chūnjú curses under her breath and frees up slack on her thread by tossing the two skycups as high as she can. She dodges the hurtling skycup in time to avoid her op-ponent scoring a point. The skycup skitters as it bounces off the floor, then continues spinning elegantly. Chūnjú nearly fumbles catching her two skycups, but they're on her thread again now, where she keeps them at speed.

Usually, her opponents wait until later in the game, when the score is more at stake, to pull off such a risky move that leaves them both open and at risk of losing a skycup. If a skycup bounces at the slightest wrong angle when it hits the ground, it can stop spinning, at which point it's out of play and cleared from the ring. Her oppo-nent, then, is the type of person who'd want to intimidate her with a powerful lead right off the bat. Rather than feel daunted, Chūnjú flares with competition. No hold-ing back. It's the finals; she can't hesitate and shy away from going on the offense.

Chūnjú tosses the smallest skycup off the thread to idle. There's a respectable distance between the idling skycups, but she and Siya have already begun shuffling around the octagon-shaped ring, rendering any sense of territory or ownership over the skycups irrelevant. She won't risk throwing the smallest skycup, which adds three points to any strike, but the medium one—worth one extra point—seems like a safer gamble. Siya's thread is empty, forcing them to be on the defensive, but that makes catching a strike that much easier. Still, Siya's gaze is fixed on Chūnjú like a challenge, and their guard remains close to their chest.

Siya's aggressive offense leaves them open to unexpected and agile strikes. Chūnjú whips her thread around to launch the medium skycup in a curve toward Siya, who hardly has the time to turn before the skycup strikes them in the ribs, earning Chūnjú three points.

Undeterred, Siya ignores the skycup, which clatters to the ground and falls still. The referee whisks it out of play as Siya deftly scoops a small skycup onto their thread. At the same time, Chūnjú makes a mad dash to scoop the medium and large skycups onto her empty thread. Siya hurls their small skycup toward Chūnjú, who jumps up to dodge it. The skycup whizzes by under her feet. Chūnjú lands and is just about to fire back when she hears a *clink!* She looks down just in time to see the small skycup jittering away from her foot before it settles into an idle spin.

Dammit. Siya must have banked it off the ring. Four points. The extremity shot usually isn't worth it, but the small cup's bonus made it a worthwhile effort. Chūnjú catches the path of Siya's gaze and launches the large and medium skycups toward them, hoping to disrupt their dive for the idling small and large skycups beside them. Chūnjú's large skycup knocks the small one out of play, then settles into a balanced spin, while the medium one strikes Siya's torso, then falls to the ground and goes still. Chūnjú 5–Siya 4.

Siya springs up with only the large skycup on their thread and an inferno of fighting spirit in their eyes. They fling the skycup at Chūnjú, then rush to scoop up the remaining small skycup, just as Chūnjú darts around the other way to pick up the large skycup. The flung skycup is grounded, leaving only the small cup on Siya's thread and the large one on Chūnjú's thread in play.

"Twenty-second warning!"

It's now or never. Siya's still got their sides open, and their entire focus has shifted to clawing out as many points as they can via an offensive maneuver. Chūnjú goes for another curved throw. The large skycup slams right into Siya's ribs, staggering them. When the small skycup whizzes off their string, Chūnjú's heart skips a beat. She leaps out of the way—but not quickly enough.

Clink!

The skycup ricochets off Chūnjú's other brace. As the buzzer sounds, Chūnjú does the mental math.

"Liola 7–Goren 8!"

The spectators erupt into a cacophony of cheers, chants, and jeers. As Chūnjú retreats to her coach's side for the minute break between rounds, she catches Siya's gaze. Unable to stop herself, she cups her hands around her mouth.

"I'm just getting started!" she calls out.

Siya grins and shouts back, "Me too!"

———

The Heavenly Feet inspection squads form during Chūnjú's last year of secondary school. She is seventeen and cramming for exams when the first officer arrives on campus, dressed head to toe in imperial Skylander garb. He takes a broad-footed stance, hands behind his back, as he makes his announcement.

"By imperial decree from Tiānkyo, all girls must unbind their feet," the officer says, sparking murmurs of dissent. "The foot is the vessel through which the Bǐyìniǎo makes their presence known. It is to be respected and left in its natural state—not modified according to earthly whims."

Chūnjú glances sidelong at her best friend, Líng. They share incredulous looks, each glancing at the other's impeccably bound feet. Chūnjú wears leather shoes like those popular in Bethana, while Líng has Tiānkyo style slippers on.

"We will be conducting routine inspections to ensure the edict is enforced. It is the opinion of the Tiānkyo Court that the bound foot, in addition to being a desecration of the Bīyìniǎo's image, is also an economic detriment to the colonies."

"Maybe we'd be better off if the Skylands didn't take half of what we make," Jiāng jeers from the back of the classroom, sparking nods and murmurs of assent. "Just admit you need us to make your food and clothes because you can't make them yourself. Then maybe we'd have some respect for Tiānkyo."

Chūnjú laughs along with her classmates. The Skylands are openly disdained in Liola, especially in Kartang, the strongest seaport, as well as the one most deeply gouged by imperial taxes. The very act of sending an officer here is an invitation for mockery.

"Why do you even care about our feet?" Miǎo says, kicking her bound feet onto her desk to whoops. The crystals on her foot wraps sparkle. "I thought you're all about modesty. Censored too many dirty magazines up there, so you've got to obsess over us now?"

The official's expression doesn't change, but color rises to his cheeks, especially as he avoids looking at Miǎo's feet. The taboo of leering at a woman's foot is multiplied tenfold in the Skylands, where all feet are unbound, and the mere thought of a bound foot is forbidden.

"Just quit now," Chūnjú says, speaking up sympathetically. "Don't you have more to do with your life than take orders?"

Later, as the squads grow more powerful and brazen, Chūnjú often finds herself thinking back to that moment. When she'd looked closer, she'd noticed that, beneath the trappings of intimidating military gear, the officer hadn't been much older than she was. In his early twenties at most, looking every bit as uncertain as she'd felt. But with every passing moment, he grows away from that hesitant boy into a cruel man who'd drink unceasingly from the gourd of power. He cares only about denying others the right to be their true selves. Even if Kartang, like much of Liola, is matriarchal, he is happy to raze all that to make way for the patriarchal governance of the Skylands. As his squads levy fine after fine on her, Chūnjú's desire to *be*, simply as she is, without this outsize obsession on her feet—as if that is *all* she is—pushes her to not only bind her feet more tightly into the golden lotuses her mother never achieved, but also to craft brass lotuses that render all production-based arguments against her obsolete.

She will beat them at their own game.

Facing off against Siya is a true battle—the kind that opens Chūnjú's eyes to the capabilities of the spirit.

The two players are tied in the final round. The energy of the crowd is unbelievable. The collective emotions crackle like lightning through her.

Liola and Goren have always had a strong animosity toward each other, even if they are formally recognized as one country on two islands. That's the only thing that lets the Skylands exploit them the way they do without creating all-out war. If Liola and Goren were distinct nations, perhaps they would ally to turn against the Skylands together. But with their nationhood only recognized as the collective of two states, exploiting Liola only serves to profit Goren, who, in turn, is only too happy to spread the Skyland Empire's doctrine in return for a secure standard of living.

The crowds have undoubtedly begun to channel the political aspect of the match. Chūnjú really hadn't wanted this to happen—*anyone but Goren*, she'd thought as she watched the brackets—but it seemed the world was conspiring to make the rebirth of the Calebriad the biggest spectacle in living memory.

"Set!"

Sweat drips down Chūnjú's brow. She's ready to spring up the instant the ref calls *go*, and when he does, Chūnjú and Siya both idle their large and medium skycups and thread the small skycups, revving them to speed. Siya feints a strike, but by now Chūnjú is getting a sense of their body language and calls their bluff. There's no more time for Chūnjú to be hesitant or to make anything but an aggressive offense. With a confident swing, Chūnjú releases the skycup to bank off the wall at waist-level right as Siya hurls their skycup in an arc. Chūnjú jumps back, dodging the skycup, as Siya dives to the right, also dodging her strike successfully. One of the skycups stays upright, but the other wobbles and clatters to the ground.

Chūnjú doesn't even catch her breath before she's sprinting toward the remaining small skycup. Siya is closer. Chūnjú doesn't think. She releases one wand and flings the thread out like a whip to wrap around the small skycup. Chūnjú catches the released handle and accelerates the skycup. Siya falls back to pick up the large and medium skycups behind them. They waste no time throwing the medium one at Chūnjú, then banking the large one. The ring is chaos, skycups whizzing as Siya darts over to pick up the medium and large cups that Chūnjú is also going for. Desperately, Chūnjú banks the small skycup, but it misses Siya by a wide margin.

Siya's and Chūnjú's eyes widen as the two realize too late that they're about to collide. They tumble together, a mass of limbs that knocks away the skycups, grounding them both.

"Foul!"

Siya and Chūnjú struggle to their feet as the judges deliberate which side was at fault. The energy in the stadium reaches a teeth-chattering buzz like that of summer cicadas. When the foul is called for Goren, Chūnjú's stomach drops as fans begin to boo. Siya's expression sours as well.

"Can't we just get on with it?" Siya grumbles. "Clearly an accident. I don't want a necroed cup."

The judges place three tokens, each marked for the three cups that have been grounded, into a shaker, then reveal that the smallest skycup will be put back into play. Siya looks offended when the judge hands them the skycup.

"Go!" the ref says, making a chopping motion before jumping back. Immediately, Siya idles the revived skycup, prompting boos and displeasure from the Gorenese fans. Then, they stand tall and nod toward the other idling small skycup.

"Let's do this right," they say.

"Agreed," Chūnjú replies.

They both dash toward the skycup, passing the spinning large and medium ones. Chūnjú flings out one handle like she did earlier just as Siya leaps. The handle smacks Siya on the arm before it whips around the skycup, which Chūnjú pulls back to her possession. Immediately, the referee calls another foul for Goren.

The first fistfights break out as the match goes on time-out for the judges to deliberate. Then, someone throws a bottle, shattering it and drawing blood. Within seconds, a massive brawl sweeps through the arena as spectators from Liola and Goren turn on each other.

The spectators closest to the ring upend their seats and advance toward the judges.

"Um," Chūnjú says. "The clock's not running anymore, I hope?"

A fire breaks out in one corner. With horror, Chūnjú catches sight of someone tumbling over the rails from the upper boxes, then another. That's what she'll never forget: the unbelievable *speed* at which everything descended into chaos.

"I'm out," Siya says, putting down their thread and sky-cups. Chūnjú does the same.

"As far as I'm concerned, this was a draw," she says. The referee has long since stopped paying attention to them. Glancing back with panic at the encroaching spectators, the referee jumps out of the ring and disappears into the masses of people.

Chūnjú bends down and unlatches the power knob on her braces. She turns both up to their maximum. The pneumatics normally give her step a slight bounce. Chūnjú jumps experimentally. Now, she leaps a good fifteen, twenty feet into the air.

"Siya, right?" Chūnjú says when she lands, amused by their awed expression.

"Yep. Chūnjú?"

"Mm-hmm."

Siya flashes a grin, their bright eyes taking in the events around them as if already calculating a battle plan.

"Friends?"

"Enough to get out of here," Chūnjú replies, smiling at Siya in turn. "Come on."

She gestures for Siya to climb onto her back. As they bound through the burgeoning riot, Siya's astonished laughter pierces the sky.

~

The skycup falls.

"It seems so frivolous," Anima says, picking it up. Ær fingers dance over the smooth edge and heft the weight of the spindle. Æ turns it experimentally. Pale blue, like a cloudless sky, edged with brass.

"Yet it's not," Vessel says, gently taking the cup from ær and stowing it back into the qíjìtáng. "Sport is ideology in a microcosm. Rules about respect and cooperation."

"A microcosm?"

"Everything in the world is made up of smaller parts,"

Vessel says. "Every big problem stems from something we can trace back to our day-to-day lives. There is a method to this madness, I assure you."

Vessel smiles.

"I shall return at forthlight. Until then, please, Anima. Take care of yourself."

———————

Anima falls through the never-ending fractal cascade of the Gleaming. The flash of entrance gives way to seahorses and glittering plumes of light spiraling out as æ falls into the endless iteration. It is like free diving, holding on to the pearl of ær individual identity as æ plummets through.

Æ can't remember the last time æ played, whether sports or games, simply for the pleasure of it. Æ lets ærself play in the Gleaming—lets ærself drift and watches how ær presence distorts the fractal sea, changes the shapes unfurling from ær. Whispers of feeling flutter through the Gleaming, caught in fleeting verse that flits past Anima like silent owl feathers.

> *so moved by love*
> *I allow myself to weep*
> *so moved by love*

I wipe away the tears
   so you don't wake

Tenderness fills Anima, a yearning as a susurration of intimacy rises. Æ recalls a profile, half-shaded, chiaroscuro bright; a glowing ember; acrid burning, forming itself into elegance.

smoke
   shaped
   by your tongue
      into love letters

Normally, Anima would push aside wants. Center ær-self on ær purpose, refocus on ær breathing, detach ær-self from the world to protect it. But in this free dive, Anima lets the feelings come—doesn't shy from their full intensity. Loss. Loneliness. And the feeling that surprises ær the most: anger like a plain on fire, slashing and burning through ær core. Resentment, hot and fatal as lava, a pressure that builds up in ær heart under the weight of duty and obligation.

Anima has chosen to subsume ær identity with the Hub in pursuit of a loftier cause. But æ can't help but wonder now if the sacrifice is parasitic. If there could be another way for æ to honor ær duty while also experiencing the full range of everything human. Of not just service but also play, formless and free.

With a deep breath, Anima leaves the Gleaming.

––––––––

suicide

Anima has handled suicide alerts before. The standard procedure is to de-escalate, and the techniques have been successful in Anima's experience. The suicidal impulse is fleeting; stalling the person is typically enough.

Æ takes the body of a day crow. Only they and the night ravens allow ær to speak directly to people. Anima prefers the rigid biometal of the day crow. The night raven is all energy and leaves ær with a sense of incorporeality whenever æ borrows the form, as if the background of stars in space bleeds through into ær body. The day crow, by contrast, is clearly delineated, solid, the pneumatic tubes hanging from its underside countable.

The feather foils cut through the air as Anima glides over to the citizen. She is to the northwest of the island, where the tame, green terraces give way to a patchwork of swamp and marsh along the estuary.

"Citizen," Anima says, amplified voice resonating past the crow's polished beak. "Halt."

The girl is pale, somewhere in her mid to late twenties. It takes Anima only a second to parse through ær records and match the face to a name: Juniper Hešeri. Prior encounters flash through ær mind: Juniper as a young child, alone in a home unlit but for a single lamp in the bedroom, its light too feeble to penetrate the encroaching darkness. Juniper, older now, arguing with her father, then storming off from the house for the last time. Juniper in a place of her own, fevered writings and sketches haphazard on her desk, her internal life something she can control and keep consistent, even as everything else around her begins to fragment. Juniper greeting customers with a smile and carrying on as if she has no bitter pain to express.

In Ora, citizens are given the right to die peacefully. Any suicide filed in advance with the Hub is vetted to ensure the decision has been made with care and consideration. This kind of impulsive suicide, though, calls for intervention. Anima glides through the last few hundred feet to stop and tread the air before Juniper.

"What is your name?" Anima says, despite having a profile of Juniper's entire life in the periphery of ær mind. The question serves to stall and ground the subject.

"Juniper," she says.

"Juniper," Anima repeats, the voice of the day crow tinny and raspy. "What is your business here?"

"I'm answering my calling," Juniper says. "Let me do this."

"It would be against my oath of safety."

"You don't understand."

"The wellness exchange can match you with a sage who can help you navigate whatever it is that afflicts you now."

Anima cannot enter Juniper's mind, but æ can still unlock a one-way neural valve between them to bear some of the brunt of whatever is happening in Juniper's mind. But as soon as æ does so and the brain waves hit ær, æ feels as if a wall of seawater has crashed against ær and tugged ær into its undertow. The energy passing through ær is erratic, manic, jumping from state to state as it courses through ær. There is pain there, and there is grief and sorrow, but there is also a mad hope, a logic to the world that makes everything significant. The energy rattles through her, giving her power, drive, the confidence to follow through where doubt had stopped her hand before. If Juniper had wings, she would be taking flight; if Juniper were a fish, the restless energy would be propelling her undulating body to the ocean horizon.

But she stands, only human, nothing but the pulses of energy radiating from her being to indicate her mental landscape.

"Please reconsider," Anima says, voice steady. "Your judgment is compromised."

"If there is one thing I know," Juniper says, rounding on ær, "it is that I can make decisions for myself, no matter how poor."

A fault line runs along her, from the nape of her neck to her waist, each moment growing wider, howling with the tunneled wind of a gorge.

"I am a sacrifice for the world," she continues. The energy releasing from her is powerful as a backdraft now, forcing Anima to beat ær wings harder against the unseen current. Anima layers a neural lens over ær glass eyes. The world goes dark save for the flashes of light crackling over Juniper's brain like a storm, throbbing with energy begging to be released, like tides slamming against cliffs. It is both terrifying and awe-inspiring. The neural lens usually shows ær a more barren landscape, pitted with hollows, sparks of thought circling the same ruts and grooves. But Juniper's mind is chaos, unpredictable, even as the play of light and patterns holds a beauty in itself, something that can be tamed and channeled.

But she needs a lifeline to reel her back if that terrifying majesty is to be witnessed by anyone but ærself. Juniper has turned her back to ær as she makes her way through mud and tall grasses into the pools and eddies of the marshes leading to the Hăilèi Sea.

Anima cycles through several more de-escalation techniques, but they only seem to harden Juniper's resolve. Anima sends a ping through the Gleaming for backup. Two of the eight nodes in the inner sanctum of the Hub run homeostasis at any given moment. Anima hopes that at least a couple of the free-running nodes are able to divert themselves from their duties to assist. Juniper's brain flashes so fast and quick that Anima has to take off the neural lens. The world fills with light again, and Juniper is once more a solid figure, nothing observable but her exterior.

She wades deeper into the grasses. Anima curses, ær ping unanswered. Æ has to do all æ can ærself.

But the day crow doesn't have much in its arsenal to stop Juniper. The night ravens have biotoxins available to pacify people in crises, but something about them has always left Anima feeling uneasy. There is a degree of trespass there different from the sonic and other sensory arsenal the day crow has for crowd control.

Anima releases the day crow and propels ærself high. Æ senses the presence of a golden jackal nearby and dives into its body. Æ darts out from the tree cover to bound through the reeds and grasses of the marshes, ær body lithe. Still, the few moments it took Anima to return in this form have put distance between ær and Juniper, who has cleared the margin and is wading into the sea, every step carrying her farther from the city.

Underwater grasses catch Anima's paws. Æ snaps at

them, tearing away blade after blade, yanking tangles out by the roots. By the time æ's extricated ærself, Juniper is up to her waist in the cold waters of the brutal sea. Still, she's close enough to haul back to shore if Anima can get a hold of her. Anima lets out a desperate howl, throat unable to articulate human words.

Juniper turns. The image imprints on Anima, vivid, immutable: waves crashing blue black, thundering past Juniper, who stands anchored even as she becomes more insignificant the more she's swallowed by the sea, her lips parted as if to say something more, her short hair, cut in a wavy bob, plastered to her cheeks like strands of kelp.

The death itself is quick. Juniper releases her footing and lets the violent currents do the rest of the work. The jackal can navigate the marsh, but it's useless in the open water. Anima makes a desperate move and splits ær consciousness into hundreds of pieces to dive into a school of fish. Æ pushes through the nausea hitting ær psyche like a brick and instead darts around to search for Juniper, the ley lines along each fish's side sensing every micromovement of the other fish in the school and of the currents carrying them. The will needed to keep ær focus while commanding a school is exhausting. Æ has to make the most of every second.

Æ spots Juniper nearby, ghostly sunlight blanching her skin pale and wan. Despite the calm she had embodied stepping into the sea, she struggles and thrashes now, all of it distressingly violent to Anima. Æ darts through the water and brings ær shimmering bodies together, trying to create a wall of scales to buoy Juniper back to the surface.

The maneuver works—up until another vicious current breaks the school up and flings Juniper deeper into the water, tumbling and disorienting her. Her limbs give out from exhaustion as she struggles to even point herself upright.

Anima tries again to no avail. Desperation chokes ær, cascades through ær veins as Juniper is dragged away once more. There's nothing else in the waters that can be of more help. The rodents aren't adapted to the strength of the water here, none of the birds can carry enough weight to be of use, and the dolphins and whales in the distance are too large to navigate these waters, which, for all their danger, are still shallow. Enigma has arrived on the shore, eir presence a shining dot, but Anima doesn't know how long it'll take Enigma to get to ær side, or if æ even has that time.

Juniper's limbs go still. Her body goes slack as she stops fighting. A powerful surge of energy ripples through the valve Anima hasn't yet closed between them. It is as if æ is witnessing the supernova of a soul: a pressure front of time and place sweeping out from Juniper's epicenter, relieving the crushing pressure of that neural storm. Ær heart sinks as æ fights the currents once more to try to save Juniper.

Æ cannot give up. Duty dictates: if not the life, then the body. The currents go still for long enough for Anima to push Juniper back to the surface and ease her toward the shore. Enigma has taken the body of the golden jackal that Anima had previously borrowed. E gets a firm grip on Juniper's collar and drags her onto firmer ground. Once æ's certain Enigma has the body, Anima explodes from the school of fish, lingering formless in the Gleaming for just long enough for ær consciousness to pull back together. Exhausted, Anima plummets back down into the body of another golden jackal and pads over to help Enigma. Æ cannot rest. Not yet.

By the time æ's back at Enigma's side, it's too late. Æ nudges Juniper's lips with ær wet nose: no sign of breath. Nor a pulse when æ presses against the jugular.

Fury steals over Anima. Æ leaps up, paws landing solidly on Juniper's sternum as æ pounces again and again, pumping at her chest. But she doesn't respond, nor does she cough up any water. She remains still. Unresponsive.

"It happened in seconds," Enigma says, voice gentle in Anima's mind. "You did your best."

The jackal cannot cry, not in the way humans can. All Anima can do is pace the shore, tail swishing with agitation.

"If I could have—I don't know—watched her more closely—"

"You can't save everyone," Enigma says. "In the end, the only person who controls what someone does is that person themself."

"She just seemed so happy to die," Anima says, stopping to meet Enigma's eyes. "To rid everyone of her. They're usually sadder."

"I know," Enigma murmurs. "Anima. Close the valve."

Æ does, severing any last link æ has to Juniper. Æ closes her eyes with ær snout. Then, as Enigma comforts ær, nestling eir head against ær shoulder, Anima throws ær head back and howls.

———————

Vessel appears again in the evening. By then, the events of the morning seem surreal. As if they'd been a dream. Unreal. Imagined.

But when Anima closes ær eyes, again and again, it is that image of Juniper in the sea looking back at ær.

"Something troubling you?" Vessel says. Anima lets out a mirthless laugh.

"*Troubling* is not quite the word."

"Then what is?" The sound of the qíjìtáng opening is becoming familiar, even if witnessing its majesty continues to stir wonder in Anima.

"I don't know," Anima says. Tears sting the corners of

ær eyes. "*I don't know.* I've never doubted my role. My duty. But now . . ."

Anima swallows. No, it's all too fresh still to put into words. Instead, æ strides over to the qíjìtáng and runs ær fingers along the rosewood until æ comes to a curious bundle of letters, each one heavy with spirit.

"Please," Anima says. "Tell me about these letters. Tell me who wrote them."

"Of course," Vessel says. Se unfolds the first sheet and begins to read it aloud.

~'

The Sky and Everything Under

Court of the Burning Sky, Tiānkyo
Date of hearing: Shuāng 64 · Hǎitáng 3
Date of decision: Shuāng 64 · Hǎitáng 8
Accused: His Majesty Duarch Sumi

Order:

1. This order shall decide the trial of His Majesty Duarch Sumi ("Accused") for high treason, as defined in Article 5 of the Charter of Ashes, through aiding and abetting

in the failed Shuāng 63 · Nata 8 coup.

2. General Sīmǎ Haimuna petitioned the Supreme Court of Kartang for a trial of the Accused for the offense of high treason. The matter was sent to the Tiānkyo High Court with jurisdiction over the entire Empire of the Skylands to investigate. Dragoman Mulabe of the Tiānkyo High Court and representatives from Liola and Goren, the Mugrosan Lowlands, and the People's Republic of Bethana agreed that there was a case against the Accused. The Court of the Burning Sky received the formal complaint on Shuāng 63 · Nāta 28.

3. Summary of the trial: The Accused appeared before the Court on Shuāng 64 · Hǎitáng 3. The formal charge was read as follows:

   ◦ Firstly, on Shuāng 63 · Āmǔ 2, you met with representatives from the terrorist organization the Aeroground Legion (AL) and divulged classified state secrets that were later used to coordinate an attack on the Imperial Palace.

   ◦ Secondly, on Shuāng 63 · Āmǔ 27, you knowingly allowed Luk Wing Chong, leader of the AL, access to the restricted Imperial sewer district, providing an entry point for the coup.

   ◦ Finally, on Shuāng 63 · Nāta 8, you used keys provided by the AL to produce ciphertext leaking defensive maneuvers during active attempts to contain the coup.

4. The Accused professed innocence on all counts and claimed trial.
5. *Evidence provided:* The prosecution provided several documents to support their claim against the Accused. A full list can be found in Appendix 1.
6. After five days of deliberation, we find the Accused guilty as charged. The Accused will be hanged until dead.
7. If found dead prior to hanging, the body of the Accused shall be taken to the Plaza of the Suns in Tiānkyo and be hanged for eight (8) days.
8. The record of this case will be stored with the Court Registrar in accordance with the Archives Act of Shuāng 22.

We vote unanimously to hold the Accused guilty of high treason and authorize his execution.

Magistrate Ānmò of the Black
Mansion, Niú Dynasty
Magistrate Xuān of the Vermillion
Mansion, Zhāng Dynasty

Magistrate Yántài of the White
Mansion, Máo Dynasty
Magistrate Kāng of the Azure
Mansion, Wěi Dynasty

Shuāng 64 · Monà 2

Your Royal Majesty,

This one must thank Your Royal Majesty again for recommending a promotion to general. Your humble servant has been taking the responsibilities here at Bāděng Outpost with utmost seriousness. The Empire may have been weakened by the colonies' defamation, but the arrow of time stays true, and we need only to bide our time to recover.

Still, it is your humble servant's opinion that we may yet be able to accelerate that course and quash any potential obstacles, as it were. If the people call for their voices to be heard and for more democracy, then why not humor them? Call it a Bureau of Investigation. Allow the people to project onto it their visions of justice and representation, even as the Imperial Court remains the only power able to appoint people into the Bureau. The ultimate authority remains with the Crown. We need not take any action—merely create the artifice that we are implementing the people's suggestions. Enough will be quelled for the people to turn an eye away from their criticism. May your humble servant suggest a revival of the Games? They have always been known to rally the people.

Now, it may be the case that such a Bureau would be tasked with investigating even Your Royal Majesty. This one humbly advises not to treat such an intrusion as an attack on the power of the Crown. Your Royal Majesty will need to cooperate, if only to gain the trust of the people. They must believe that the Crown can be molded into their image. Humor them as you would a child, if only so the child behaves. Remember: only the image of penitence matters. When it comes time to craft policy, allow the Imperial Court to beautify the words. The scholars can obfuscate the true policies Your Royal Highness authorizes so a commoner would not know the consequences of such an edict.

It is your humble servant's opinion that the

traitorous Sumi will fall soon enough. Your humble servant's people are diligently searching for him. He may claim to speak for the people, but he will find soon enough that people are simply too small-minded to care. Without the authority of the Crown, he is nothing but a criminal. Can such a pipe dream of an idea as a world without the duarchy move the hearts of so many that they will indeed labor to build such an absurdity, all while the Crown that serves them, provides them food, water, work, transport, is right there supporting them already? Such concepts as "nation" and "governance" are beyond the reach of peasants who must eat and merchants who must sell. The masses are simply too disparate for Sumi to have any hope of uniting them.

Bādĕng is in the heart of the Firetide Margin. The trees and chaparral here may be destroyed by a wildfire, but the seeds they drop need that very heat to signal when it's time to sprout. So too is the Empire: We can only rise from the ashes once we have already burned.

Loyally yours,
General Zhào Wǔxī

EMPIRE OF THE SKYLANDS BUREAU OF INVESTIGATION

RE: Interview with His Majesty Duarch Koto on Shuāng 64 · Monà 28

MAGISTRATE HYO: My deepest thanks for taking the time to speak with us today. I am Hyo Pingso, Magistrate. And this is Detective Van del Boh Nam. Ms. Yoshi Hong Chew will be transcribing today's interview.

DETECTIVE DEL BOH NAM: It's an honor, Your Majesty.

HMD KOTO: The honor is mine. I am humbled by those tasked with enforcing the law of our empire.

MAGISTRATE HYO: Yes, yes, all for the greater good of the empire. Let's skip the honorifics and make this as quick as we can. We're on the brink of chaos as is.

DETECTIVE DEL BOH NAM: Please, Magistrate Hyo. Have some respect.

HMD KOTO: It's quite all right. I understand.

MAGISTRATE HYO: How would Your Majesty describe Your Majesty's relationship with Duarch Sumi?

DETECTIVE DEL BOH NAM: Your Majesty?

HMD KOTO: I apologize. It often takes me a moment to collect my thoughts.

MAGISTRATE HYO: Take as much time as necessary.

HMD KOTO: Sumi and I—we were close, at first. We had been found very quickly in succession and bonded through our childhoods. Up until we ascended to the throne in the summer of last year, I believed we were confidants with no secrets between us. But—I have learned much about deception recently. I will say that much.

DETECTIVE DEL BOH NAM: Did Duarch Sumi ever confide in Your Majesty the intent to undermine the Crown?

HMD KOTO: No. No, never. Hence my abject shock over . . . recent events.

DETECTIVE DEL BOH NAM: Understandable. Your humble servant is certain Your Majesty is now aware of Duarch Sumi's escape and current fugitive status.

HMD KOTO: Yes. The press doesn't sleep, unfortunately.

MAGISTRATE HYO: We have people stationed in Tiānkyo, Lichen Chasm, Kartang, and all along the Firetide Margin. As of now, His Majesty Duarch Sumi has evaded capture.

DETECTIVE DEL BOH NAM: Your humble servants would greatly appreciate it if Your Majesty could provide insight on where Duarch Sumi may be hiding.

HMD KOTO: Ah. I—I have been posting letters to Sumi with Mīdden, one of our homing birds. Although I am unable to determine his exact location—he has not responded—I know that he has received them, as Mīdden returns empty handed.

MAGISTRATE HYO: A homing bird? That would certainly help.

HMD KOTO: Yes. I suppose so.

DETECTIVE DEL BOH NAM: Your humble servants understand that Your Majesty is close to Duarch Sumi and that the bond between duarchs cannot be understood by anyone but other duarchs. Still, this is a matter of state and empire that transcends individual duarchs.

HMD KOTO: Yes. Yes, you are right.

MAGISTRATE HYO: We can't spare any more time on sentiments. Surrender Mīdden to us.

DETECTIVE DEL BOH NAM: Please remember that you are still speaking to our ruler, Magistrate.

MAGISTRATE HYO: We've already had one go bad. Why not both?

HMD KOTO: I assure you, I am invested in the survival of our empire. Please, follow me. I will fetch Mīdden.

MAGISTRATE HYO: We appreciate it.

HMD KOTO: Here she is. Please treat her with kindness.

MAGISTRATE HYO: We'll be in touch again if we need anything further.

HMD KOTO: Ah—before you go—one more question.

DETECTIVE DEL BOH NAM: Yes?

HMD KOTO: Is there any possibility that Sumi's sentence can be commuted?

DETECTIVE DEL BOH NAM: Your humble servant cannot advise on that.

HMD KOTO: I understand. Thank you again for your service.

Shuāng 64 · Sòng 4

My dear Sumi,

It has been five days since you were declared a fugitive. I can no longer send Mīdden out in search of you. But I write you unposted letters still, in hopes that you will read them someday, in hopes that you will know I have never once stopped thinking of you.

As the lotus blossoms rise from their muddy depths in the courtyard's pond, I wonder where you are—resplendent, surely, against any backdrop. They have been calling me a one-winged emperor, which I find excessively dramatic. But it is a fitting title, given that the last time a ruler held the crown alone was a hundred years ago.

I suppose it's easy being a one-winged emperor when I know little of any other way.

I miss you, Sumi. I miss you every day. Your touch, your voice, your presence, the closeness we had. I know you have your ideals and your convictions. Is this what you wanted?

I wish for your swift return and an end to this instability.

With love,
Koto

---

③ is a symbolic gesture. The Royal Mint represents the capital that the Empire has accrued at the expense of civilian lives. Currency represents our promise that we will honor the monetary value of that capital. But when we divest from that illusion, we can

⑥ The naval border is strongly policed, but the Black Cliffs to the north of Liola are little defended. There is an existing network of abandoned mine shafts that converge at Pángǔ Pass. We

⑨ are cycles. We must be willing to fight for peace. War is temporary, but a world where self-determination and autonomy are our fundamental rights can be permanent. Institutions of oppression can and do collapse to be relegated to the past. Our future

---

Shuāng 64 · Mùběi 23

My dearest Sumi,

My heart has been torn by your absence, but I know you are still alive. Our souls are entwined—my body would know of your death.

The Aeroground Legion has bombed the Kartang Mint and laid siege to its remains. How naive I was to think that simple tests for explosives would be enough! While my best officers were patrolling government buildings with dogs in search of gunpowder, terrorists posing as employees entered, one after another, with flour hidden under their coats—plain, ordinary flour that can be found in any home. But get enough finely sifted flour in the air of an enclosed space like the Mint, then light a match . . .

It is an insult in itself, the absurd simplicity of their method. Then the Aeroground Legion had to make a public spectacle and declare their use of flour as some symbol of the worker, or agriculture, or whatever rhetoric they wish to wield this time. A nuisance. Can the people truly be trusted to govern themselves when they turn immediately to violence to make a statement that is, at best, incoherent?

The willows trail their leaves in the river as the second sun sets. The bed is too empty without you, Sumi. Come home.

Yours,
Koto

Shuāng 64 · Chuí 8

Your Royal Majesty,

This one is overcome by Your Royal Majesty's

trust and confidence. When it seems that even the Imperial Court begins to turn on itself, know that your humble servant continues to be faithful to the Crown. The duarchy has existed for hundreds of generations, and it will exist for hundreds more. The doubts and fears Your Royal Majesty expressed show not weakness, but the heavy burden of a ruler.

Allow this one to dispel the notion that the Crown is fallible. The Skyland Crown is manifested upon the duarchs by the Convergence. Your Royal Majesty was born with the feet of a bird—the divine touch of the Bǐyìniǎo. Not only that, Your Royal Majesty identified the mementos of the prior duarchs, proof that the Convergence has bestowed upon Your Royal Highness the wisdom of generations of the duarchy.

The Convergence is absolute. To question it is to question the very force that keeps the Skylands afloat. It is the one power that is infallible.

The duarchy, however, was never meant to be borne by one ruler. The burden of power has always been meant to be shared by two, in the image of the Bǐyìniǎo. Unfortunately, the search for the next duarch cannot proceed while Sumi is still alive. The Crown, once manifested, cannot be surrendered or bestowed upon another. Only with Sumi's death can another duarch manifest.

This one cannot possibly fathom the sentiments Your Royal Majesty has for Sumi. But it is the opinion of your humble servant that it would be best to sever those emotional ties early. Harden the heart now, if only to spare it the eventual heartbreak upon Sumi's execution. Perhaps the Games will provide enough of a spectacle until then.

Loyally yours,
General Zhào Wǔxī

Patient admitted Shuāng 64 · Chuí 11. Patient was in attendance at a skycup match when a disputed referee call turned into a politically motivated riot. Patient has defensive wounds on palms and contusions on torso. Rearfacing talons have been broken off at second knuckle. Recovered digits were trampled beyond recovery. Wounds immediately cauterized. Patient states she was targeted for her harpy feet. Evidence of persecution submitted to Bureau of Investigation.

———

Shuāng 64 · Chuí 12

Van,

I told you the time would come when we'd have to get tough. We've already got people renouncing their Kumoi citizenship. They weren't content moving to Haneul or Niyangniya or Tengeriin or Dēr, either. They're taking airships down to that godforsaken island on the surface.

Well, let them go into exile. See how long they'll last under absolute anarchy. With the Crown weakened as much as it is and riots continuing after that damn skycup match, it's going to be left to us to police the people.

I know you believe in what the Crown symbolizes, but I'm asking you to be realistic. Look around you. The people out there rioting and looting don't care about the Crown. They care about feeding their kids and providing for their families. You have to admit that the Crown has been doing a shit job of that.

We're in a position to change that. We're right at this moment where we can get the Bureau to represent a new nation instead of the Crown. With a shift in authority, the Bureau can topple the Imperial Court and enforce laws that actually improve the lives of our citizens.

Still, people will be people. Be prepared for things to turn ugly. You may be a pacifist, but I'll be armed at all times. Nothing worthwhile has ever been born without a little bit of blood.

—Pingso

THE KARTANG STAR

Shuāng 64 · Nāta 5

THE FALL OF THE SKYLAND EMPIRE

Teo Hak Fu

The reincarnation cycle of the duarchy ended twice: first at 15:17 upon Sumi's execution, and again at 16:26 with Koto's formal renouncement of the Crown. With the Imperial Court dissolved, the Empire of the Skylands, those ever-present tracts of land in the heavens casting their shadows upon us, has ceased to be. The Federated Union of the Skylands takes their place. Among the first words spoken on behalf of the new nation were those disavowing the burgeoning city-state of Ora below, comprised of exiles from all over the Skylands, including a significant number of refugees from Tiānkyo.

Reactions to the end of this era have varied...

———————

Shuāng 65 · Kōba 1

My dearest Sumi,

Happy new year, beloved. I wish I could do more than just lay flowers on your grave and pour a libation for you. How you ever managed to drink báijiǔ, I'll never know.

There is so much about you I will never know.

Mīdden is again by my side. I have taken her to your grave, too. Perhaps it is a kind of bliss to not recognize death even when it is before you. Perhaps to Mīdden, you are simply no more.

I can never think of you that way. Even if it pains me to see my ever-growing stack of unsent letters, another part of me knows that your spirit lives on in them, captured in the ink of my love.

I may yet be reborn. We may yet reincarnate and meet each other again. The Convergence still exists outside the Crown; that much is true. But now that I am not a duarch but one of the people, I shall live as they do—with the expectation that life is finite. I will be buried next to you, and everything we are and were, every complexity, every contradiction, will be from then on forever unknowable.

Yours now as ever before,
Koto

~

"What is all this?" Anima says, shaking. "Why do you subject me to tragedy and death?"

"Don't you find something to learn within?" Vessel asks. "A glimpse of something bigger than you?"

"Do I need to feel such pain to learn?" Anima says, tears in ær eyes. "Such sorrow?"

"So you feel pain upon hearing of these people's lives."

"Yes," Anima says, turning away. Æ clenches ær fists, stiffening ær shoulders as æ hides the hot tears running down ær cheeks. "Too much, maybe. I soak it up. Soak it in. It becomes part of me, and it haunts me. What I see in the city. What I see in the mementos."

"Isn't that a treasure in itself?" Vessel says gently. "To feel it all?"

"It's a curse," Anima says, spinning on ær heel to face ser. "I am exhausted, Vessel. I give and I give. I give until even the boundaries of my body are gone. I give, and I ask nothing in return." Æ chokes back a sob. "Nothing but to be helpful. To better our broken world. Yet I can't even do that."

"Anima," Vessel says, making ær look up. It's the closest æ's stood to Vessel. Se is a palm or so taller than ær, and se scents the air with a warm and sweet perfume. "I don't know what's made today so difficult. But the pain is bigger than just this story. That much I know."

Se puts the letters back onto their shelf.

"Have you ever felt like this before?" Vessel says. Se keeps a respectful distance from Anima, who finds ærself longing for the first time in a long while to have someone sit beside ær—to be with ær as two people, one offering the other a shoulder to cry on. But even if æ may long for it, Vessel is still a stranger, one with whom Anima doesn't feel comfortable broaching the topic of touch. Æ maintains ær distance as well as æ replies.

"I don't . . . I don't think so," æ says as æ sifts through ær memories. "I've felt great sadness. I've witnessed terrible things. But I don't know what this feeling is. I feel like I've been torn open and something more powerful is trying to come through, bigger than I could ever contain."

Æ shakes ær head, a bit too hard. Ær neck twinges with the force of it. Normally, æ would abscond from the intensity of such feeling by retreating to the Gleaming. But Vessel is here, and it would be rude to run away from ser. Anima tries to quell the feelings, but finds that they intensify the more æ tries to quash them.

"I don't know how to make these feelings go away," æ says, voice trembling as the pressure mounts and tears escape ær eyes. "There's no neural valve *I* can open for relief."

"What exactly happened today?" Vessel asks. Without any prompting, Vessel hands Anima a soft, lace-edged handkerchief that matches the lavender robe se's wearing. "Maybe talking about it will help."

"I can't," Anima says. The handkerchief seems almost too fine to desecrate by blowing ær nose into it. Æ attempts to leave the minimal amount of mess on the soft silk. "It's—I'm not ready to."

"I understand," Vessel says, nodding. "Maybe you can write something down instead. Whether truth or fiction, that has always helped me. It doesn't so much remove the pain as it domesticates it into something you can coexist with."

"I can't remember the last time I held a pen," Anima says, unclenching ær fists. "The last time I put anything down in ink."

Vessel laughs.

"Where I come from, anything lasting must be written in ink. Spoken words are too fleeting to rely on. And they change over time."

"The Gleaming is our archive," Anima says. "Every record that needs to be retrieved is stored within the consciousness of the Hub. Writing is what is ephemeral—destroyed easily by fire and water."

Anima's gaze lingers on the bundle of papers. Even the drag of a vine would be enough to tear the paper—some sheets are so thin that they are translucent. Fibers that absorb pigment in patterns that somehow produce significance. Yet there is something undeniable about their realness, their presence. Something to holding them, boundary against boundary, that calls forth a deeper unknown than the boundless Gleaming, ever expanding, ever able to preserve more. Whittling away at words as if to carve away meaning and reveal truth—Anima scans over the handwriting again. Some of the strokes are delicate and refined, others coarse, every hand shaping ink differently. The individuality of it makes ær head spin.

"You do still have pen and ink here, don't you?" Vessel asks, smiling. "Or has that, too, become obsolete?"

"No, we do," Anima says.

"Why not try it? Just pick up a pen. Put it to paper. See what comes out."

"I—" Anima begins, then pauses. It's not true that æ has too much work to do. Æ's been put on homeostatic processes for the foreseeable future—at least a month, perhaps two. Standard protocol for any node who has witnessed death in the line of duty. There is no better time to try something unusual than now.

And perhaps it would quell the dull roar pounding against ær eardrums.

"Just try it," Vessel says.

Later, when the room is empty again save for ærself, Anima leaves ær pod. The room is bare. Walls carved with decorative molding lead to the moon gate, where thick clusters of wisteria and lace lichen surround the circle like a shawl.

Æ takes a step past the moon gate, one hand to the stone of the frame, ær stem floating through the air behind ær. The stem limits ær movement, keeping ær close to the pod, with the trade-off that all of Anima's biological needs are fulfilled. Æ has shelter and care here, duty and purpose.

"Excuse me," Anima says, flagging down an attendant. "I would like paper and pen, if you'd please."

"Of course."

Anima watches as the attendant turns the curve and disappears. It is always eerie to ær how ær requests become commands to others. It is a power that comes along with being one of the eight nodes of the inner sanctum, yet it still feels arbitrary. Undeserved.

The paper the attendant provides is finely woven hemp. She also hands over an elegant dip pen and a bottle of black ink. Anima thanks the attendant, then waves a hand to form a smooth writing surface and seat.

Anima touches the nib to the paper. An ugly inkblot blooms. When Anima tries an experimental stroke, the line extends only briefly before the nib catches, scratching the paper and splattering ink everywhere.

Rather than feeling frustrated, Anima is surprised to find that the tactile feel of it keeps ær pushing the pen simply to see a trace of ærself in the world. A line following in ær wake.

Anima pauses. Isn't sure what comes over ær when æ touches pen to paper again and writes:

Juniper Hešeri

Juniper's face appears in ær mind's eye. Certain. So convinced of the decision she'd made. Æ matches it back to the archives, tries to follow the palimpsest back to her birth. Writes the date down. Wonders what else æ could write in between—that she always smiled when greeting a customer? That she loved to eat candied hawthorns? That her mind was a place of terrible beauty, raw like a wound and brimming with as much life?

But all of that is only the briefest glimpse. When æ touches the pen to paper again, it is only to write her date of death.

"You have to stop coming back here."

Anima turns, flicking ær forked tongue to taste the air. Æ has borrowed the body of a monitor lizard, its scaly and rough hide impenetrable, its formidable size and power a deterrent to the other animals, who keep their distance. All except one: a squat frog splashing through the water to approach ær. Enigma.

"Why?" Anima says, looking past the reeds and grasses to the turbulent Hǎilèi Sea.

"You need to give wounds time to heal," Enigma says, coming to a stop on the muddy edge of the estuary, where Anima has been sitting in the suns since midday. The first is sinking fast below the horizon. The second, larger sun follows at a slower pace, in a wider arc. Ruby and gold tones blanket the marshes. For a moment, the crashing sea turns a rich scarlet, brilliant, as if to remind ær that ær own blood is water, too.

"By hiding?" Anima says, flicking ær tongue out again. The monitor lizard can smell carrion several miles away, but Anima doesn't catch the scent of a human body here.

Not anymore.

"No," Enigma says. Eir tongue darts out to snap up a passing fly. The monitor lizard's vision diminishes with the light, but even so, Anima catches Enigma's dark eyes glimmering in the golden light. "By forgiving yourself. By moving on. By giving yourself the space to live your life. The good you do ripples out to others, Anima."

"What good?" Anima says, standing, ær heavy tail beating back the reeds in agitation. Enigma, tiny as e is in the frog's body, stands eir ground, even as Anima's tail whips dangerously close. "I don't know what I'm protecting anymore. Why prevent Orans from seeing Skylanders? History? Are politics worth separating families and lovers for? What good is a city built on such morality if it can't prevent one of its own citizens from killing herself?"

The grasses rustle. A dark-brown mink peers out, startles upon seeing Anima, and darts back into the reeds. Enigma snaps up another fly. Anima considers going after the mink, but ær human nausea over blood and death overrides the lizard's instinctive drive to feed. Æ lets the mink go free.

"It's not our job to create a painless society," Enigma says, hopping closer. "It is our duty to create a society that provides for its citizens. A society where no one is invisible, where we can meet the needs of every one of our people. There are those who would encroach on that. Protecting our people means protecting our sovereignty."

"Is this the right way?"

Enigma croaks, as if e is laughing.

"Who said anything about right and wrong? This is simply our way. I choose to serve these principles with every decision I make. But," Enigma says, hopping over to a stone and looking up at Anima with an unwavering stare, "I can only make that decision for myself."

Enigma catches a dragonfly. In the dying light, Anima can only glimpse the delicate glimmer of the membranous wings, the glittering facets of the dragonfly's two large eyes, all folding in on itself as Enigma swallows the insect. Anima tastes the air again out of habit, noting that the mink is now several hundred feet away. Æ still doesn't have an appetite. Although the frog's expression remains the same, Anima senses Enigma's gentle smile.

"You shouldn't keep your visitor waiting," e says. "Go on. Don't come back here."

With that, Enigma is gone. The frog leaps into the reeds. Anima digs ær claws into the mud, takes one last look at the sunset, and returns to ær body. The amniotic bath doesn't soothe the churning knot of feelings in ær gut, and ær hands shake as æ pushes apart the fronds. Æ composes ærself as æ steps out to greet Vessel.

"Good evening," æ says, nodding. As if sensing the residue of a lizard mind on ær, the snake perks up, floating and flicking out its forked tongue.

"You've seen much lately," Vessel says, peering into Anima's eyes. Ser dark eyes reflect every hint of light. Ser gaze is intense, even if Vessel doesn't mean to scrutinize.

Anima looks away and nods.

"I have."

"Many of these mementos are difficult to witness," Vessel says. "Most are not happy. Not even positive. You are not obligated to browse them, even if I am here."

"What is life without its traumas and pain?" Anima says. "I—" Æ hesitates, then continues, surprised by the unfamiliar certainty in ær voice, "I *want* to. There is so much more in the world beyond this city."

Æ circles the qíjìtáng. So many objects. So many stories, so many lives—too many for ær to witness completely. This time, æ lets ær eyes pass over the flashy, colorful items like the marionette and the skycup and the obviously personal effects like the letters. Instead, æ selects the most unassuming object ær eyes land on: a single fish scale, not even a pretty color—just a dull gray.

"You are certain?" Vessel asks.

"Yes," Anima replies. Vessel keeps ser gaze on Anima for a moment longer, as if to verify Anima's intent, then nods and places the scale in Anima's hand. The soul in it is faint. Just barely perceptible. But it grows stronger as Vessel begins to speak.

~

As Dark As Hunger

The sun bears down hot and twisted against the nape of Ellen's neck. She wades into the muddy waters, slick, yellow-brown silt clinging to her worn rubber boots. The rotten scent of fish hangs heavy in the air, which is loud with the buzz of flies and the shrieks of cicadas.

Summer here is an oppressive season, sick with humidity. The river floods, then washes back sewage and garbage. As the water recedes, the muddy pools evaporate. Any fish able to survive the reek of dank, infested waters die by suffocation on dry land. Then the gulls, the crows, the carrion-feeders pick at the corpses until they're nothing but bones bleaching in the sun.

The fans Ellen keeps running in her house on stilts do nothing to calm the heat or drive out the stink. The most they do is add a low, humming drone that keeps the whine and buzz of insects at bay. Still, Ellen never begrudges the flood season. She knows where the cleaner waters are, where, with her hands covered by thick gloves as she holds a pail full of bait and a net, she can seed the shallow waters and catch fish without even needing a line. The fish are enough to keep her fed. The work leaves a sheen of sweat on her that traps every sour, marshy scent of the river to her skin.

Ellen drops a catfish into her bucket, where it thrashes for a few moments before playing dead, the only movement the flutter of its gills, opening and closing like butterfly wings. Just one is enough to last her the whole day. She'll gut the fish, always careful to avoid puncturing the bitter gallbladder, then use the whole animal, usually in a stew or soup. She even grinds the bones to use as fertilizer for the small garden in her yard.

Before she can turn and trudge back to the shore, something catches Ellen's eye. There, beyond the leaves, half-hidden by the thickets of mangroves rooting the path of the river, lies a shining, smooth fish tail—a massive fish, larger even than the sharks sold at the wet market. As she watches, the tail twitches once, twice, then beats against the muddy bank, a wet *slop-slop* sound, the earth underneath slithering and squelching.

Something must have gotten caught in the mangrove roots during the flood. Ellen sets her bucket on the banks beside her, tugs her boots higher, and wades out toward the thing, her movements steady and her expression calm despite the ever-quickening beating of her heart and the sensation of her throat closing.

Another thrash. The silvery scales give way to flashes of skin not white enough to be the belly of a fish. Instead, it's the rich yellow-brown of her own skin. She's never seen mermaids in her time here, but her grandmother had told her stories about them. Ellen recognizes the form as it emerges.

With every step Ellen takes, her body drags through the water, leaving chevrons in her wake. The surface dimples as water skippers skim away from her, and little bubbles break the surface as fish dart up to eat the algae and insects floating on the surface like gasoline.

When she comes around the last bend, Ellen stops. The tail of a fish flows seamlessly into the torso of a young woman, her arms threaded through mangrove roots. Her long, black hair, slimy with algae and the waste of birds that had roosted above her, is tangled in the branches.

"Hello?" Ellen says, her voice hoarse. When she reaches out, her fingers tremble. "Do you need help?"

The stench of the river mixes with the iron of blood as Ellen takes another step. The mermaid's back is to her. She's caught in the mangrove roots as if they were stocks, her head locked facedown as she struggles. Up close, what Ellen thought was a shadow turns out to be dark smears of blood slicking the silt on the banks.

Another thrash of the mermaid's tail reveals the source of the blood: a gash runs along her abdomen, piercing where a navel would be on a human. The wound is deep enough to reveal the glisten of her intestines. It's a wonder she survived, never mind that she still has the energy to struggle as she does.

"It's okay. You're safe now," Ellen says. She unsheathes her machete and hacks away at the roots, getting one arm loose and then the other, always conscious of where the blade is so she doesn't add to the mermaid's injury. She works more carefully around the mermaid's head, aware of how the mermaid is breathing too quickly and the way her shoulders are stiff with tension.

When Ellen whittles away the last of the roots shackling the mermaid, she whips free, riled up with adrenaline and panic, and tries to take off back into the water. But as she twists toward the water, she cries out and clutches her abdomen, her palms slick with blood.

"You'll die if you go back in there," Ellen says. She's speaking in the most widely spoken tongue, but the mermaid isn't responding. Whether she doesn't know the language or is simply too shocked to speak is unclear. Ellen steps toward the mermaid, her boots squelching in the mud, and pushes aside dripping locks of matted hair to take a better look at the mermaid's face.

She freezes. Her mouth goes dry. The furious eyes that glare back at her are eerily familiar.

The mermaid has her face.

Ellen splashes back to the shore and returns with her boat, her chest heaving with her labored breaths. She ties a few knots with old hemp rope around the mermaid, who yells at her, teeth bared, the gills under her jaw flaring open and closed. The language sounds familiar, but Ellen doesn't understand what the mermaid's saying.

"Hush. You'll feel better soon."

Ellen drags the mermaid onto the boat, the knots binding her tail neat and practiced, restraining but not cruel. Her muscles burn with the effort. The mermaid flops onto the boat with a *thud* rather than the slippery *thwack* Ellen expects. Her tail quivers in its readiness to thrash. The engine of Ellen's boat sputters and throws clouds of black smoke into the air as she sets off for her house again.

As the boat skips over the waves, Ellen glances over at the mermaid again, who's glaring at her with the fury of both suns. The edges of the wound are clean, too deliberate to have been a propeller accident or an animal attack, and the way the mermaid's skin sags reminds Ellen of the stray cats who've given birth to litters and litters of kittens, their stomachs now hanging low and empty. A couple specks of bright orange linger against the red of the mermaid's flesh.

As soon as she's docked the boat, Ellen hauls the mermaid hand over hand into her home, leaving a slick trail of blood, grime, and slimy algae water leading from the back sliding door to her only bathroom, where she dumps the mermaid into her bathtub and runs the water. She undoes the knots and sponges away at the mermaid.

She goes into the closet and pulls out a spool of her heavier thread and her sharpest needle. With an experienced hand, she stitches the edges of the mermaid's flesh together, closing the wound. The point where her body transitions from human to fish is strange, firm in a way that feels uncanny to the touch. Ellen's hand hovers over the scales of the mermaid's tail, fingers quivering with longing. But her heart holds her back, telling her that this isn't an animal to examine, but a person to treat with at least the most basic of dignity.

"Can you speak Common?" she says after she ties off the last stitch, carefully avoiding eye contact. With the mermaid's hair washed, detangled, and combed back, Ellen gets an even clearer look at her face. There's no doubt about it—the face is decades younger, but unmistakably her own. Even though the water running over her hands is warm, goose bumps speckle Ellen's arms as revulsion and fear run through her.

"Huì shuō Mǔyǔ ma?" Ellen says, switching to her second tongue. When there's no response, she switches to her third. "Eske ou pale Kreyòl?"

Still no response, not even a grunt or a gesture that suggests she understands. Hesitantly, Ellen tries a phrase in another language:

"Si gisurembi Gisun?"

The creature takes a deep, rattling breath, then exhales. If Ellen hadn't known what to listen for, she would have missed the mermaid's reply.

"Inu."

The mermaid breathes out a few more words, but they're beyond Ellen's knowledge of Gisun, which she knows only through a few battered children's books and the long-gone creaky voice of her grandmother. She does, however, know how to ask one more question.

"Sini gebu ai sembi?"

The mermaid relaxes a bit, as if finally sure Ellen is on her side. When her eyes meet Ellen's again, the fight has gone out of them, leaving her looking tired and defeated.

"Kiru," she says.

"Kiru," Ellen says, tasting the name. Kiru watches her

wordlessly. Then, Ellen puts a hand over her heart and says, "Mini gebu Ellen sembi."

Kiru offers her a small smile.

"Hojo na, Ellen."

Ellen awakens the next day to the sound of propellers—a ship is making its way up the river toward her. But this one doesn't sound like it's from around here. Here, Ellen normally hears sputtering, dilapidated boats like her own, red-rusted and sun-faded.

She dons a shirt and a loose pair of pants before stepping outside. There are no government symbols on the ship, just neatly stenciled names. Ellen makes no move to greet the sailors, even after they dock. People don't usually come to the wastetides on good terms.

A tall, slender woman leads the entourage off the ship. She's the kind of lean that comes with years of practical experience, her bearing more tigress than human, her clothing pragmatic and efficient. Her belt holds a few sheathed knives of different sizes, and Ellen knows there are more knives hidden elsewhere on her person. The woman's eyes shine golden amber in the hazy morning light. As she steps off the boat, she toes aside seaweed clinging to the walkway and wrinkles her nose. The gesture is almost imperceptible, as if she's trying to hide her disgust, but Ellen knows that face too well to miss the gesture.

"Can I help you?" Ellen says, her voice steely and cold. She's a good head shorter than the woman.

"Ellen," the woman replies. Her voice is husky, lower than what her features might suggest.

"Stella," Ellen says, acknowledging her only that much before moving on despite her body's memory: trembling, warm, sweat-drenched. Her eyes flick to Stella's blades, then back to Stella's face to find Stella watching her intently.

Ellen says again, "Can I help you?"

Stella sighs. "I suppose I shouldn't have expected anything different."

Ellen lets the remark pass. Stella gauges her reaction. Then, she continues.

"Mermaids are returning to spawn," she says. Ellen keeps her expression neutral. She'd closed the door behind her, blocking all lines of sight to the bathroom, and the house is quiet, but Ellen still has the uneasy feeling that somehow, Stella knows about Kiru.

"Why should I be concerned?" Ellen says. She places her hands on her hips, taking a more open, offensive stance, but it's a bluff—her heart pounds furiously against her chest, and her palms are slick with sweat. The briny, green scent of algae growing on the river's surface rises along with the wet stink of the whole place. Somewhere deep in the mangrove thickets, a bird cries out. Stella tilts her head and gives Ellen a simpering smile.

"I would have thought that *you* of all people would take an interest," Stella says. Ellen flushes, heat rising to her cheeks and churning in her gut, indignation and shame together as one.

"You've got quite the gall to show your face around here again," Ellen says as she shakes her head. "Just get to the point."

Stella's smile doesn't falter, but her eyes narrow, giving her smile an edge of malice.

"They're paying good money for mermaids," Stella says. Ellen's skin prickles, her stomach dropping in anticipation of what Stella might say next.

"Who?"

Stella considers Ellen for a moment. She buffs her nails and glances at them. Ellen doesn't have to see them to know that they aren't yellowed like her own, with dirt perpetually wedged under them.

"Despite how you may feel, you know much of the rest of the world sees mermaid as a delicacy, and they fetch spectacular prices on the open market," Stella says. She raises a hand to cut off Ellen's protests. "The reality is that the demand is there, and my crew and I would like to try more humane ways to meet it. But we need more mermaids to start with. They only come back to spawn every twelve years, and then only for a few weeks at a time."

"So let them be and leave me alone," Ellen says, turning to go.

"A hundred thousand yi," Stella says, stopping Ellen in her tracks.

"Excuse me?"

"That's how much a live one fetches at the market. More for certain qualities—brindled mermaids are said to be particularly delicious." The opacity of Stella's smile has Ellen uneasy with how she can't be sure what emotions it represents. "But even if the pay is generous, I know your interest in them, too, Ellen. We have the equipment you don't have to get close enough to a school of mermaids and take them in alive and unharmed. The most you can do by yourself is get close enough to see a flash of scales before the mermaids scatter and disappear."

Ellen thinks of Kiru and is about to retort that she doesn't need Stella for that, but she catches herself in time. She doesn't want Stella to know about Kiru—the very idea makes her tremble.

"They're not killed," Stella says, eyeing Ellen's balled fists before meeting her eyes again. "That much has been outlawed. Their tails are just cropped, not unlike a dog's.

They adapt to that easily. The process has become quick and preserves as much of the mermaid's range of motion as possible. They say the tail doesn't feel pain anyway. And a hundred thousand yi is payment for just one mermaid. Hundreds come during a spawning season. You know this river and their ways better than anyone else here, I'm sure of that."

It's an attractive offer. It wouldn't be much to assist Stella, and she could think of a number of uses for that much money. She could escape the stinking river once and for all, for instance. Really make something of her life and herself. All she'd have to do is something the rest of the world does anyway.

But then she thinks of Kiru and imagines the horror of having part of her body severed. The mermaids may survive the whole thing, but, Ellen thinks, living things survive all kinds of pain and cruelty.

"I'm not interested," Ellen says. Stella's expression doesn't change, but she looks Ellen in the eye longer than Ellen feels comfortable with.

"Well, it's your loss," Stella says at last. "If you do change your mind, though, we'll be docking at Ermei Village. Come find me."

With that, she turns on her heel and boards the ship again. Ellen crosses her arms and glares as the ship sails back to the fork in the river and disappears.

Still, when Ellen goes inside and opens the bathroom door, watching as Kiru stares at the ceiling, gills only barely flaring open and closed, she can't get Stella's last words out of her mind.

Come find me.

She and Stella had had their time together. Their relationship had been explosive and passionate, barbed and toxic. Even after they'd gone their separate ways, she'd still thought of Stella. Healthy or not, happy or not, Stella was a lot of Ellen's firsts, including her first love.

Ellen had taken in every detail of Stella. She'd looked youthful, her face hiding her age, even if her hands had shown it. And her hands had been bare. No rings or bands. Just the familiar calluses where the handles of her blades have kissed skin so often it's turned to stone.

Ellen closes her eyes and touches her forehead to a doorframe, grounding herself as she lets out a small sigh. They're different people now. It would be foolish to expect something Stella's never willing to give.

Kiru's shallow, labored breaths punctuate the silence. Disquiet settles over Ellen as she takes in features that are indisputably hers—the uneven dip of the lips, the mole under one eyebrow, the upturned nose—yet completely foreign. She can't help the uneasy fascination, like the first time she'd locked herself in a room with a mirror and truly taken a look at every part of her body. Strange, uncharted topographies lie before her.

Even if Kiru didn't have her face, Ellen would still have done all she could to save her. Her grandmother's stories of their mermaid ancestors remain precious in her heart. Even though she may be only human, to take Stella's offer feels like a betrayal.

Ermei Village.

Ellen leaves the bathroom door ajar behind her. Kiru's breaths whisper through the night.

It takes three days for Ellen to gather the will and resolve to go to Ermei Village. She'd fought with herself the entire time: true, she's the best to navigate the mangroves, but that only affords her more of a chance to actually find and catch mermaids. Could she mutilate one to satisfy such a horrific craving? It happens, she knows that well enough, even with the very people around her—those who'd spent longer in the wastetides tend to respect the mermaids' spawning season, but newcomers are more unscrupulous and not only sell mermaid tail at the market, but have also begun to clear the mangroves for other profitable ventures.

Ellen doesn't know if she can treat living beings as strictly business like that. But, at the same time, the stagnation of the wastetides is slowly choking the life out of her. This could be her one chance. Stella *had* mentioned being humane to the mermaids. Visions of a house in a city thick with the smells of rain and street food, or a cottage in the countryside where she could wake to clean dew and the sweet perfumes of flowers outside her window, grow stronger as they become more of a possibility.

She heads to the main part of town: the hawker center, where dozens and dozens of food stalls serve people late into the night. Even though there are still many people around at this hour, it's far less crowded than usual. Ellen spots Stella finishing the last of a bowl of steaming noodles at a table.

"Changed your mind?" Stella says as soon as Ellen sits across from her. That had been one of the things she couldn't stand about Stella—the way she held herself over others, as if she always knew more or knew better.

Ellen doesn't fall for Stella's bait. First, she goes over to a stall and returns to the table with a cold drink, sweet and tangy, biding her time as she lets the steam over Stella's tone vent from her. Then, she leans her elbows on the table. "I suppose," she says.

Stella smiles.

"I've thought about you a lot," Stella says. "I know we argued. But we always found a way to make up for it."

Ellen flushes. She remembers the raised voices, the

charged emotions, the way she would retreat and sulk for days, nursing her wounds. The way she'd go back into the room, ready to share a bed with Stella again, who knew as much as she did that it was the most of an apology either of them would get. And then Stella would touch a kiss to her neck, and that would be enough to mend her heart; and then Ellen would ask for Stella's hand, *one, two, three*, and that would be enough to mend her soul.

Ellen is a hard woman, stoic and straightforward; the emotions she shows are earned. Stella is the opposite: the slightest emotion manifests itself in her expression, and she polishes that into brilliance with her charisma. But when it had been just the two of them, they could cross each other's walls, reversing roles, reversing personas. Whether either was "the real Ellen" or "the real Stella" had often crossed Ellen's mind, until she eventually settled that both parts of her were real, and neither part of her was real.

"I need strict boundaries if I'm going to work with you," Ellen says as she sips her drink. Moths flutter against the lanterns hung throughout the hawker center. The sound of sizzling starts and stops like a round. "One: you tell me up front if you want something out of me. Two: you tell me the entire truth."

Stella looks taken aback for a moment. There's a second when Ellen isn't sure if it's the flicker of the lights or if anger truly flashes over Stella's face. But when she blinks again, Stella's face is soft. She nods.

"I understand."

She places a hand on Ellen's. Ellen's skin tingles, pinpricks of sensation blooming. Her breath catches.

All these years, and her body still reacts the same way to Stella's touch.

"We leave at first dawn. The mermaids usually spawn during forthlight, so we'll need to be at a good fishing spot before then. I'll see you tomorrow."

She gives Ellen's hand a squeeze, then pushes her chair back and stands. She downs the rest of her drink and sets the glass on the table.

"I'll need to get some rest tonight. I'm glad you came to me, Ellen."

It only hits Ellen when she's back home on the porch smoking that Stella had been the one to come to her.

"The whole truth," she mutters, then pinches out the rest of her cigarette. The screech of cicadas cuts through the muggy air. She toes off her slippers at the back door and steps inside. Her bare feet pad down the hall to her bathroom, where she kneels beside the bathtub.

Kiru's scales have lost some sheen, and her skin looks waxy. Ellen reaches around her tail. With effort, she pulls the plug. The hollow, whirling sound of the tub draining reverberates off the bathroom tile. The water that swirls away is yellow brown, blood mixed with dust and silt mixed with the grime of the river.

Ellen fishes out the clumps of hair slowing down the drain and tosses the wet, soap-globby tangles into the trash can. She rinses Kiru off. The edges of Kiru's wounds have begun to stitch together, but it's too early to see if she has any signs of infection, and Kiru is still too weak to help Ellen bathe her and tend to her wounds. Kiru winces in pain, crying out words in Gisun that Ellen doesn't know. She takes care to be as gentle with Kiru as possible while Kiru clenches her teeth.

Better than death, Ellen tells herself.

She puts the plug back in and draws another bath. Steam suffocates the room. As the water runs, Ellen goes to the pantry and rummages through the shelves. She returns to the bathroom with a few packets of dried herbs and powders. She places them under the faucet and throws in a couple of handfuls of salt for good measure. She could choke on the smell of the bathroom: blood and waste and medicine.

She doesn't open a window, though. With the steam trapped in the bathroom, Kiru does seem to regain some shine and vigor.

Kiru speaks again, her voice wetter this time, but Ellen still doesn't understand a word other than a couple of the most basic ones.

A part of her gives way as tears come to her eyes. She reaches out and holds Kiru's hand. She'd expected her palm to be clammy, but it's warm like hers. Kiru's fingers twitch as if to try to squeeze Ellen's hand, but her breaths are still shallow, and her body is limp.

"I'm sorry," Ellen says. "I don't understand."

Ellen's grandmother had told her about mermaids. The harpies and the nagas are natural opposites: one has dominion over the sky, while the other rules the earth. But the kitsune and the mermaids are opposites, too. The kitsune is a shapeshifter and can choose to never settle on one form, while the mermaid can change form in only one way, and only once: she can tear her tail in two to form legs. But, in doing so, she gives up her home in the water, and her children are born without tails.

Ellen's grandmother had told her, too, about the last time she'd seen her own father. Her mother had sat on a boulder by the shore, furious tears streaming down her face, as Ellen's grandmother watched from the pebbly shore closer to her father. She had been too young to understand the details, but she'd known that it had to do with the fear that smothered their home, the way they and the others around them had pared down their possessions to only what truly couldn't be replaced and always had plans for how to leave quickly.

"I won't stay here without you," Ellen's great-grand-mother had said.

And Ellen's great-grandfather had murmured a few words about the rest of their family and their friends needing his support—that he'd be there to join her once this passed, once this was safe. But for her to have a tail now, for her daughter to have a tail now, was certain death.

Others had hidden. She wouldn't be the first.

Ellen's grandmother never knew what made her mother change her mind in the end. But she could always recall what happened next: her mother had gripped one side of her tail fin in either hand and, with her teeth clenched, she had ripped apart the silken membranes, hissing as they'd torn from each other. Blood had dripped down her fingers, fat, red beads that clung to the boulder, forming rivulets.

Her father had done the rest of the bifurcation with a hunting knife, cutting away the tailbone, slashing away the thin sinew binding the two sides of muscle together. The fish skin would wither in a few days, and fresh skin would cover the rest of the wounds. Her mother had lain half-catatonic, raw resentment flashing across her face as she'd made eye contact with her daughter. Ellen's grand-mother had stared and stared into her mother's cold glare, until her father came into her field of vision wearing the saddest smile she'd ever seen, which soon became all she remembered of him.

"I'm sorry," he'd said.

And then he'd cut her tail in two.

Ellen's grandmother had shown her the scars. They were slight, she'd said, because she'd been young. Her father never returned, and the other mermaids went into hiding. What knowledge of Common they had dwindled as they isolated themselves more and more from the world. And when they did encounter other peoples, like when it came time to spawn, their Gisun words were unintelligible to them, leading many to believe that mermaids didn't have a real language.

And here Ellen is now, exiled from home because of events she'd had no say in. And, as Kiru lies before her—perhaps a sister or a cousin or a niece, or even some other version of herself—she finds herself unable to put together the words to ask about home. To gain the merest entry, a gate left ajar.

Ellen turns off the tap as soon as Kiru is submerged. She squeezes Kiru's hand, then stands—but as she does, Kiru closes her fingers around Ellen's wrist, startling her.

"Baniha," she says.

Ellen lowers her head and blinks a few times. Unable to hold back her emotions, she looks back up, smiling as she lets the tears fall.

"You're welcome," she says, closing the door behind her as she leaves.

───────────

The suns haven't had a chance to heat up the day by the time Stella and her crew set out on the river. The last of the night insects' chirps die down, to be replaced by the birdsong of early morning. With the horizon going gold against the dark silhouettes of mangroves and cattails, Ellen could almost call the river beautiful.

She takes Stella south-southeast. They don't find any mermaids there—their nets come up empty or tangled with algae and trash. By the third day of this, Stella gets impatient, pacing the decks after they've docked and the rest of the crew has gone. Against the darkness of night, she questions Ellen.

"I know these aren't the best waters you're taking me to," Stella says, her lip curling back in a sneer. "You've been wasting my time."

"It's hard to spot anything in the river," Ellen replies, her voice level. "And they've learned to be stealthy. I'm doing my best."

But the response isn't enough for Stella. She's worked up now, energy flashing through her. She sheathes and unsheathes one of her blades, making Ellen sweat. Stella notices and flashes Ellen a smirk. She comes close to Ellen, backing her up against the rails.

"I missed you," she says, pulling Ellen into an embrace, their bodies fitting together in a way that could make Ellen weep. Stella leans her cheek against Ellen's neck, then turns so that her lips almost touch Ellen's skin.

Ellen lets out the tiniest of noises.

"Did you miss me?" Stella whispers. She trails one hand up Ellen's chest to clutch at her throat, her thumb on one artery and two fingers against the vein, pressing like the point of a knife dimpling skin.

Ellen's breath hitches.

"Yes," she chokes out.

Stella plants a kiss against the crook between Ellen's neck and shoulder, making Ellen's knees go weak. Her breath is hot against the shell of Ellen's ear when she speaks.

"Let me take you home."

Stella hitches Ellen's smaller boat to her own. Ellen can't help but watch as Stella's callused fingers rough over the hemp rope, tying sturdy, neat knots. There's a moment when the boats are hitched together and they've both straightened up when Ellen thinks, *I could say no. I could tell her to stop. She respects that much, at least.*

But the rest of her says *want* and *need*, says *give* and *crave*.

Stella doesn't do anything on the waters down to Ellen's

home except fiddle with her blades, glancing at Ellen every now and then and smiling when she sees Ellen shiver.

"I've never met anyone like you," Stella says. The river is clear as they sail downstream, nothing but mangroves and insects around them as Stella's boat chops through the water.

"Nor have I," Ellen says, quietly. Her skin feels electric, primed to respond. It's been so long since she's been caught breathless like this, thrown into a submissive head space where she can let power fall into someone else's hands. It's intoxicating and fills her with sensation and flighty impulses, makes her head spin with the richness of Stella's scent and the brightness of her touch, tunnels her vision so that only things like *feel* and *taste* and *breathe* remain.

They dock the boats together when they reach Ellen's home. Ellen unlocks her door and fumbles for the light, but Stella knocks her hand away, laughing.

"You think I don't remember everything about this place?" she says. Even in the dark, she can manhandle Ellen around her own home to her bedroom. Ellen goes soft in her hands, her words slipping from her, replaced by sensation and docility. It shocks Ellen how quickly the change comes over her, how quickly she remembers and responds to it, even though it's been decades since she was last with Stella. How much her whole being electrifies now, craving and remembering.

"Let me see them," Stella says, her breath hot against Ellen's skin. Ellen sits on the edge of the bed while Stella kneels, arms propped up beside her. Ellen hesitates, but only for a moment. She unzips her boots and sets them aside, then pulls down her pants and tosses those aside, too.

"They're almost gone," Stella says, coming closer to Ellen's bare thighs. Her skin isn't as youthful now, and the scars have mostly turned white, but a few browner marks remain: scales etched and woven by a blade, each as wide as a thumb, the whole lacework spanning the fronts of her thighs.

"I . . ." Ellen says, then takes a breath. "I miss them."

I miss you, she wants to add, but doesn't. Stella gives her a knowing look, as if she hears the words anyway. She unsheathes her knife and presses the blade against Ellen's skin. Ellen shudders—the blade is fine and cold, but Stella holds it so that it doesn't break skin.

"They don't have to be gone," Stella says. She runs the point of the blade up Ellen's leg, spiraling to nip at the inner thigh. Ellen hisses, but her skin is only red with a pinch.

Ellen had never shared her wishes with anyone until she met Stella. She'd hardly been able to express them to herself, the way her body didn't feel real, the way parts of her always felt alien and wrong. How she'd never managed to bring the blade to herself but knew that having the blade put against her, dragged against her skin, leaving smears of blood—that it would help, somehow, to see the scales carved into herself; that the pain of having her blood revealed to herself would bring her exhilaration, make her body quake and her heart race in ways that nothing else would.

And there had been all the times when, filled with fury and rage, her mind overwhelmed with voices, Ellen would stare into the distance, seeing only her internal vision: her skin flayed from her body, ribbon after ribbon pulled back to reveal what she was inside. She would stand still, unobservable to the outside world, her skin prickling and crawling with the need to be ripped off, with the base desire for destruction.

Only Stella had understood. She was crisscrossed with scarred sigils and seals herself, her skin readable in the dark. By whose blade, Ellen was never sure. She'd never asked.

It had become ritual and release, inversions and subversions of power, a place where Ellen could be truly inside her own body with all its pain and pleasure and blood. She'd never seen it as mutilation, but sacrifice.

But the two of them were like fire and wind, each goading the other on, passion and fury, heat and explosions.

Twenty years and Ellen had tried her best to come to peace with herself, to learn her own topography and begin to see her body as a home instead of a collection of unfitting parts, as true in itself, as a skin to inhabit and not to shed. To grieve for the places she could never go to, the doors shut long before she'd arrived.

Impulse pounds through Ellen. In the end, she's still in the same place: facing a door and unable to read the sign. Familiar fire salts her skin, makes her want to tear everything away in her overwhelming, unarticulated grief and fury.

"Six," Ellen says.

Stella smiles.

The blade runs quick over her. Ellen gasps as her skin pinches apart in the knife's wake. Blood beads up big and wet. Stella's hand is deliberate around the curves of the six scales. Ellen is alight with sensation, her body throbbing with it, exhilarated with the high. Tears well in her eyes, cathartic and hot, her body aglow in the ritual and feeling.

Stella strokes Ellen's skin, her hair, the unbroken skin of her other thigh, and waits for Ellen's breathing to steady.

"Let me clean you up," Stella says. She stands and leaves the bedroom. Too late, Ellen snaps back to her senses, her head rushing with whiplash.

"Stella, wait—"

But Stella's opened the bathroom door. The bed creaks as Ellen gets up, blood trickling down her skin as she dashes over, her stomach dropping as she sees Stella staring straight at Kiru.

"Well," Stella says, her eyebrows raised as she turns back to look at Ellen. "I thought we were telling each other the whole truth."

Ellen mumbles, trying to string together a sentence, but Stella waves her hand as she turns back to observe Kiru.

"Whatever. I don't care about the how or the why. I only care that this one got away. Thankfully, it's still alive."

Words come back to Ellen as her throat opens up again.

"You can't take her."

Stella laughs. She squats down and looks at Kiru, who sneers and spits in Stella's face. Ellen's eyes widen as she braces herself for a fight, but Stella calmly wipes the spit off her cheek. Kiru's chest heaves, her nostrils flaring as she stares down Stella, who turns back to Ellen and gestures at Kiru.

"And what will you do? Keep it here or in some miserable pen until it dies anyway? Might as well make the last of its days comfortable."

Stella stands. She hooks her elbows under Kiru's

shoulders. Kiru thrashes, protesting Stella's handling, but she runs out of energy quickly, her ribs heaving as she pants, her gills a bruised purple red. Stella lugs Kiru out of the tub. Kiru slips and lands with a wet *thud* and a shout. She slides herself back, but Stella starts dragging her again by the arms and hair.

It's uncanny, seeing Stella handle Kiru with such force. The rage on Kiru's face is palpable as she claws back at Stella, who doesn't flinch. Ellen wonders if that's what she looks like when she, too, is filled with rage. She wonders if Stella sees the resemblance, whether it thrills or horrifies her if she does.

Ellen can't tug Kiru back; she'd probably injure her further. She tries reasoning with Stella, then prying her grip off Kiru, but Stella is stronger than Ellen, her hands like stones. Stella drags Kiru across the dock and the footbridge into her ship, where she unlocks a large door to the hold and throws Kiru in, doing nothing as Kiru tumbles and screams.

Stella takes the three steps down to the hold. Bluish light casts up from the level below, mixing with the indigo black of night. Ellen descends the three stairs in pursuit, but, just as she readies herself to confront Stella, she stops in her tracks.

A tank with a few lifeless mermaids, their expressions distant, takes up most of the hold. Although her heart leaps to her throat upon seeing them, her gaze lingers longest on a smaller tank filled with orange masses. She flashes to Kiru's wound and the orange dots that she'd seen before and pieces the memories together.

"You're breeding them? Like animals?" Ellen says as she stares at the thousands and thousands of eggs, however many generations held in captivity.

Stella breaks her stride over to Kiru and shakes a lock of hair out of her eyes before giving Ellen a cold smile.

"More humane this way, isn't it? In a few generations, we'll be able to breed new varieties and improve the quality of the stock we already have. More mermaids in the wild, better product for consumers. Win-win, no?"

Kiru thrashes on the floor, the stitches along her abdomen glistening in the light. Stella heaves Kiru's tail over her shoulder and starts dragging her toward the tank. Kiru scrabbles her nails against the floorboards as she resists. The jagged, raised edge of a loose plank catches on her and pries her open, tearing out several of her stitches. Kiru screams as her wound splits open and her blood smears across the wet floorboards.

Stella drops her grip on Kiru's tail. Ellen's hands ball into shaking fists as fury seizes her from head to toe. She runs over to Kiru and kneels, holding her as Kiru sobs.

"What makes you think that's humane?" Ellen spits. She tugs off her shirt and uses it to stem Kiru's bleeding.

As blood seeps into the cloth, more words spill out of Ellen's mouth. "Maybe they won't have hooks in their mouths, but do you have any idea what captivity does to the spirit?"

"What spirit?" Stella says, looking genuinely confused. "Do you weep for a chicken's spirit? A pig's?"

"You've never understood," Ellen says, desperately trying to see through her cascading tears. "Even if she were nothing more than a fish, you must still honor her. You can't just inflict suffering and walk away like you do over and over again. Besides—"

She turns away from Stella to tend to Kiru. The entire shirt is soaked through with blood. She tosses it aside. The wound is more severe than it was when Ellen first mended it. Kiru screams again, a howl that batters Ellen's heart. Even knowing that it would add no more to her pain than the agony she's already suffering now, Ellen is still careful to wipe away her own tears so they don't drip into the brutal gash on Kiru's abdomen and sting her with their salt. Kiru's hands shake violently as she gropes for Ellen, who holds Kiru's hands in hers, as if to provide Kiru a mooring.

"Don't you feel this pain?" Ellen says, breaking down into sobs. "All those years, you told me I was the one who was strange for feeling so much. But now I know: what's strange is how you don't feel this pain at all. You don't actually care about being 'humane.' You've only ever cared about yourself."

She wipes the grime, sweat, and blood from Kiru's face, doing all she can to at least give Kiru dignity if she can't give her life. But then Kiru looks up, her eyes dazed and unfocused as she grimaces with pain.

"Mimbe wa," Kiru says. Ellen's mouth goes dry.

"What did it say?" Stella says, already squatting down and heaving up Kiru's tail again. Her nonchalance, her continued brutal manhandling of Kiru, leads Ellen to believe that Stella asks not because she wants to know, but as a curiosity, like seeing a bird do a trick.

"*She* said," Ellen says, "'Kill me.'"

Ellen darts forward and grabs one of Stella's knives. She steps back before Stella can react, her arms still full with Kiru's tail. Ellen doesn't parse the words Stella's shouting. She kneels by Kiru, mouths an apology to Kiru's nod, then, in a swift movement, she cuts Kiru's throat. As Kiru sputters, blood flowing thick and hot, Ellen reaches a hand into the slick, gory insides of Kiru's abdomen and finds a greenish, membrane-covered sac.

"Don't you *dare*," Stella says. She drops Kiru's tail. But Ellen's grip on the gallbladder is firm. She yanks it out with a slippery tear of sinew, then slashes it open with the knife and lets the bile spill over the gash in Kiru's abdomen.

"You can't take her," Ellen hisses. Bile seeps into Kiru, rendering her flesh bitter and inedible.

Stella storms up to Ellen and throws her against the wall, a hand around her throat. Ellen gasps as she scrabbles against Stella, the back of her head aching from the slam.

"Useless," Stella spits, watching as Ellen struggles for a few moments longer. She releases Ellen, who collapses, gasping. Stella heaves the lifeless body out of the hold and hurls it overboard, back into the muddy river, where it floats faceup, eyes open. The river carries the body only as far as the next thicket of mangrove roots, where it comes to rest.

Stella takes Ellen by the wrist and hurls her down the gangway to the dock. She unhitches Ellen's boat and tosses the line unceremoniously to her, then makes her way back up to her boat. She pauses to look back at Ellen.

"You owe them no allegiance," Stella says. "Get over your fantasies."

She starts her boat and chokes the sky with smoke as she roars away up the river. Ellen gets in her own boat, rides across the choppy wake, and propels herself over to Kiru. She pulls Kiru's body up to the banks, where she kneels beside her and closes her eyelids.

"Mujilen be sindaki," Ellen murmurs.

Put your heart at rest.

Ellen lets a hand fall onto Kiru's tail. She lets her fingertips trace over the scales, lets herself observe their rapidly vanishing iridescence, lets herself touch what never was. As Stella's ship disappears over the horizon, Ellen takes the last of the gallbladder bile and drips it into her six still-bleeding scales.

~

The fish scale is warm like skin in Anima's palm. Carefully, æ returns it to Vessel.

"Such a nondescript memento," Anima says, "and yet it is imbued with so much."

"Many of them are like that," Vessel replies. "Such moments are not always glamorous. May even be ordinary. But they reveal something about the spirit. Something so essential, it imprints onto these objects."

Anima bites ær lip. Picks at the lichen crusting ær nail beds and clinging to ær cuticles. Strange energy pulses through ær. It takes several heartbeats for ær to recognize the feeling as excitement.

"I think I know what I want to give you," æ says. The thought is exhilarating and terrifying at the same time, but the more Anima thinks about it, the more certain æ becomes. "But I'm not quite ready. First, I have a question for you. Then, a request."

Vessel tilts ær head, curious.

"Go on."

Anima thinks back to Juniper. How she didn't have to die. How, even as she lived, she'd always had her face turned toward death, like a flower to the suns.

"Tell me," Anima says. "How were you supposed to die?"

Vessel's expression remains neutral as se takes in Anima. Se exhales softly. The mask drops, revealing the Vessel beneath the charm: Weary. Exhausted. The pleasantry practiced, the loftiness gone. Se no longer seems otherworldly. Even the snake stops hovering and coils around ser arm like a vine on a pillar. Vulnerable core in the open, Vessel reveals serself as human—extraordinary, but human nonetheless.

Like ærself.

"Suicide. I attempted it, but right there on the threshold, I was offered a choice: die now, or complete a task to live. I was suddenly terrified of dying again. Funny how it takes facing death to realize how much you want to live. So I took the offer."

Silence settles on them for a few moments. Vessel's gaze turns downcast, but there is an edge of relief, as if it is a blessing to no longer wear the mask before Anima.

"I witnessed a suicide," Anima says, finally.

Vessel's mouth falls open. Then, to Anima's surprise,

Vessel begins to weep, the tears heavy and lustrous as pearls.

"I'm so sorry," se says.

"For what?"

"The grief," Vessel says, shaking ser head. "It touches you, too, now."

Anima swallows thickly. Is that what it is? Grief, even though Anima had no other connection to Juniper? But that's not true—Juniper is—was—part of the Gleaming as well, just like every other living being. No matter their connection, Juniper's death still ripples out to ær.

"I barely knew her," Anima says, ær throat tight. "I only saw bits and pieces of her life. Not enough to get a sense of who she was."

Vessel smiles.

"Exactly. But that is the question the psychopomp asks of every person they meet: 'Who are you?' We will never know who someone else truly is. We are still bounded by the limits of the material world. We still cannot enter someone's soul to navigate the interior sea of the mind. But we can take a moment, a story, that illuminates their spirit, if only one facet. Yet that is what makes life the brilliant gem that it is: the collection of all those facets into a prism. A lens."

"A hundred lives lived beyond your own."

"Maybe. I've considered that. Why this task? Why

must each item be given—why can't I take a hundred mementos from one person with a colorful life? Perhaps I am meant to kill only one thing: the ego. Only then am I free from the idea that any life is singular. Free to see experience as collective, lives as interlinked." Se smiles. "That makes taking any one life, especially your own, that much more difficult."

Vessel's smile is genuine, bittersweet as the tears continue to roll down ser cheeks. Anima conjures forth a bench, hanging from the tree on vines, and invites Vessel to sit beside ær. Æ takes one of ser hands in ærs, holds it palm up.

"Let me tell you about my favorite place in this city," æ says, drawing a circle on Vessel's palm to represent the bounds of Ora. "Once you return from there, I will have your memento ready."

~

the night raven leads   the day crow tails
the moon as she sets   the suns as they rise

        dawn:

   the precipice
      /

where two worlds meet

the first sun rises earlier
) not much brighter than the moon (
his light a procession
layering the earth
with forthlight's shimmering
    blue   black   orange
       translucence.

= the horizon = glows with = streaks of = rose = and
   white =

      as the second sun reveals
         her brilliance
wringing indigos ~ from the night.

harness the Gleaming
    branch yourself {
        into the eyes of a day crow:

sleek chrome / shining brass
an aerodynamic machine
glinting / camouflaging
with the sky.

  track
the movements of the city
its pulse its heartbeat
every interaction between its citizens

   circle over
    the concrete canopy

   where the buildings
    are so close
  you can jump
    from roof
     to roof
  like hopscotch.

land
 watch
beak closed
 silent
   as a citizen steps onto
   the rooftop,

   places a radio
  on spongy moss
   damp with dew,

turns a notched dial
    as if twirling a lover.

the day crow
& the night raven
  do not sing &
    nor do the pigeons roosting
    in every crevice
      of the city &

    the songbirds live
where the earth is wilder:
    where dirt alone is enough
      to grow from.

dawn sings
    in their stead :||

      counterpoint |
    weaving static-softened |
whistle and chirps |
    into a warm harmony.

stay a while.

watch

as the two suns ascend
  to their apex
      ^   he slower than she
          the train of a dress woven from light
          billowing in her wake.

when the suns reach their peak,
their song dissipates into
the soft, blue fresco of morning.

the radio hums.

  go on,
the suns say,
  turn the dial again

  let go of solitude
and return to the city.

~

Anima gathers the tools æ will need: vines twisted together into a strong rope and the sharp edge of a saw palm's frond. Æ conjures a liana chair and sits, hands folded in ær lap, stem floating through the air as æ waits.

"I went to hear the dawn chorus."

It is the first time Vessel materializes in front of Anima. The air shimmers, as if light is intersecting and refracting differently through it, and Vessel comes into being.

"It was beautiful," se says. Se takes in the tools Anima has laid out, then sweeps ser gaze to meet ærs. There is a spark of curiosity in ser eyes, but mostly ser expression is grave with the weight of ritual.

"I will give you my memento on one condition," Anima says.

"What is that?"

"Take me out of the city with you," Anima says. "That is the only way I can give my memento to you. Otherwise, this will be for nothing." Æ picks up one length of vine and pulls ær stem close. Touching it is uncanny, mixing sensory signals to create a discomfort that isn't quite pain—more the ache of prodding one's navel. Æ swiftly ties the vine around the stem, then ties another length of vine a palm away. "Will you do that?"

"Yes," Vessel says, eyes glittering. "I will do whatever you need to give us both life."

"Good," Anima says. Æ takes a deep breath as æ picks up the sharp blade of the saw palm. Ær stem swells with the Gleaming beyond the second tie; the two sections of the stem closest to Anima have already begun to dim. Whether æ is growing light-headed from the tie-offs or from the adrenaline of the decision, æ isn't sure. But æ remembers the fish scale—remembers flesh and sinew severing, tells ærself that æ can bear this, too. Before æ can change ær mind, Anima grips the stem and slices through it. The tie holds, but barely. A couple motes are already floating through the severed stem.

"Brace yourself," Vessel says. Se puts an arm around Anima's waist. Then, an unbelievable pressure closes in on them. The last memory Anima has of Ora is the vine bursting free and the severed stem filling the chamber with light.

Anima comes to in the middle of a vast plain. Bronze and copper grasses ripple out into an endless horizon, where a sliver of sea is just barely visible. A colorful city extends inland from the shore.

"This is my home," Vessel says. "The city of Nameron in the Mugrosan Lowlands, along the Firetide Margin."

"It's gorgeous," Anima says, making Vessel laugh.

"You haven't even been in the city yet."

"Still," Anima says, looking out. "I can feel it. The city's heartbeat. That in itself is already beautiful."

Anima touches the nape of ær neck. The stem is still, no longer pulsing with ethereal energy. With deft fingers, Anima ties a knot in the stem close to ær nape and tears away the remaining length.

"My memento," Anima says, cupping the drying stem in both hands as æ offers it to Vessel. There, with nothing for miles but the unfolding apex of the qíjìtáng, Anima admires the wonder room for the last time.

"Will I see you again?" Anima says.

Vessel shrugs, ser smile lopsided, tinged with a trace of fear, so painfully human.

"I don't know. I haven't exactly done this before."

"Promise me this, then," Anima says. "Next time we meet, I will trade you a story for a story. Simply for the pleasure of it."

"You have yourself a deal."

Reverently, Vessel places the cord in the last empty spot in the middle of the qíjìtáng. One by one, the mementos glow with the Gleaming, until their brilliance is too much to behold, and Anima is forced to close ær eyes against the light. Æ will be alone—truly alone—for the first time in a long, long while. There will be no Vessel, no trunk left once the light is gone.

The light fades.

Anima opens ær eyes and sees the world.

Acknowledgments

So many people leave traces of themselves on my work. I would like to thank a few people in particular who've had a major impact on *In the Watchful City*:

Future Affairs Administration and Ant Financial, for coordinating a trip with both Western and Chinese science-fiction writers to Hangzhou in 2017. The facial recognition technology I got to see there, along with the cultural differences in attitudes about surveillance, inspired me to write this biocyberpunk story.

Dorothy Ko, for authoring *Cinderella's Sisters: A Revisionist History of Footbinding*. The book formed the basis of my research for "This Form I Hold Now" and helped me create a narrative focused on agency rather than the expectations of the Western gaze.

Trung Lê Nguyễn, for *The Star Spinner Tarot*. I divined at least half of this novella using his beautiful deck, the first one I've ever had that includes Asian iconography drawn by an Asian artist. Art creates art. The auntie of the cards has spoken.

Johnny Liu, for helping me work through the details of how combat skycups would actually be played. Without his game development insight, I wouldn't have been able to create as cohesive of a sport as I did.

Danny Lore, for asking the hard questions about who does and doesn't show up in comfort work by non-Black creators. Vessel took ser final form as I thought about Danny's comments.

Jonathan Strahan, for seeing a spark in "As Dark As Hunger" and creating a path for this novella to exist. I'm still stunned that I actually *did* this. Having someone who believes in my work as strongly as Jonathan does is an incredible feeling that I treasure.

Paul Krueger, for showing me that decolonial stories are possible. You told me to write my weird, and that freed me from trying to tailor my stories for anyone but myself. My stories are so much stronger now. No matter what people remember us for, we will always have this.

Thin Mint, my sweet baby angel. Even with your passing, you gave me a gift. The grief of my first real experience with death was the final spike I needed to drive into this railroad. I'm so grateful you held on and that I was able to honor your life by giving you a dignified and safe death. You will always be my dæmon.

And lastly, Art and my family, for being there alongside me as I experienced everything that distilled into this novella. Not just the moments of terror and uncertainty, but also the visceral feeling of learning how to gut a catfish properly, the wonder of hiking through Sedona and seeing the perfect circle of Robbers Roost, and the curiosity of wandering through museums and witnessing art and artifacts that tell countless stories. To write, you must first live. Thank you for giving me that.

February 22, 2021
San Gabriel, CA

About the Author

S. QIOUYI LU writes and translates between two coasts of the Pacific. Ær work, including fiction, poetry, and essays, has appeared in several award-winning venues. You can find out more about S. at ær website s.qiouyi.lu or on Twitter @sqiouyilu.

TOR·COM

Science fiction. Fantasy. The universe.

And related subjects.

*

More than just a publisher's website, *Tor.com*
is a venue for **original fiction, comics,** and
discussion of the entire field of SF and fantasy,
in all media and from all sources. Visit our site
today—and join the conversation yourself.